STRONG
SIDE

STRONG SIDE

WALKER UNIVERSITY STALLIONS
BOOK 3

AVA SUTTON

ISBN-13: 979-8-9929966-8-5

*For all the friends who **accidentally on purpose** fall in love.
Your stories are my favorite.*

PLAYLIST
Break Up with Him - Old Dominion
Say You Do - Dierks Bentley
Treat You Better – Sean Mendes
Mirrors - Justin Timberlake
I'm Yours - Jason Mraz
Miss Americana & The Heartbreak Prince - Taylor Swift
Friends - Chase Atlantic
Wasted On You - Morgan Wallen
Girl in the Mirror - Megan Moroney
Wet Dreams - Artemas
Need You Now - Lady A
Sit Still, Look Pretty - Daya
Song About You - The Band Camino
Our Song - Taylor Swift

PROLOGUE

NOELLE

END OF SECOND YEAR AT WALKER UNIVERSITY

ONE MORE MONTH. *I can make it one more month.* This has been my mantra all day.

It's the end of not only my second semester of my second year at Walker, but almost the end of the school year at the elementary school where I student teach and volunteer for their various school programs.

Today was field day, and the chaos from the day with kids ranging from five to eleven just about pushed me over the edge. Of course, it didn't help that it was hotter than hell out there. And on my way home, I realized that I hadn't eaten at all today, and the headache that's coming on needs some immediate attention, or it'll turn into a migraine.

My cell phone rings, and I quickly glance at the display screen in my car and see that Casey is calling me. He's been my best friend since middle school and one of the reasons I chose to attend Walker University instead of Chandler State University.

Outside of school and my boyfriend, Trey, I spend the most time with him.

I tap on the screen to answer his call. "Hello, Casey King."

"Hello, Noelle James." He chuckles deeply. "How was your day today?"

"Well, I'm hot, tired, and ready for a two-hour shower to try to get rid of my headache. It was field day, so it was a long day. I went straight from my last morning class to Arrow Cross Elementary School, and I'm just now on my way home." I huff.

"That sucks. What can I get for you? Do you want me to bring anything over? I have that ginger tea you like."

This is one of the things I love about Casey. He knows me better than I know myself.

"No, I'm good. Trey is supposed to come over later, so if I can't get this headache to drift away, I'll have him bring me something."

"Uh-huh. Yeah, right. Well, let me know how that works out, and when he bails on you, just text me what you need," he grumbles.

I know Casey thinks Trey's the worst. And maybe he's right. I'm not blind. I see him bailing on me. But it's complicated.

When I met Trey in our freshman year, I was smitten. He was in my history class and asked me for my notes after the first week, then sat next to me every class afterward. Within a month, we went on a date.

Trey's my first boyfriend and first everything. He was my first real kiss. I lost my virginity to him. And he's the first guy to make my heart equally burst and hurt. Our freshman year was fun, and dating Trey was exciting. And then … well, he changed, and Casey has seen it all. He's not a big fan of my boyfriend, and nothing I say will change his mind.

"You're too good for him, Noelle. You deserve a guy who puts you before everything."

"Okay, Mr. Football Star. Like you'd put a girl before your ambitions."

"For you … I'd put the whole world on hold."

I roll my eyes at his dramatics, but my cheeks betray me with a flush. "Smooth line, Romeo. Save it for the jersey chasers."

I turn onto my street and rub at my temple. I hate talking to Casey about Trey because he has a hard time reining in his disdain.

"Case, he's been pretty good about being more attentive to me lately since they lost in the playoffs. He's just hanging around until he leaves for the summer league in Minnesota. He came over last night and made me dinner. It was sweet. We're all good." My voice hitches slightly.

It wasn't all good really. He was on his phone the entire night and barely talked to me at all. So, I went to bed, and when he came in later, he woke me up for sex that lasted maybe all of ten minutes, then immediately rolled over and went to sleep.

"Right. Well, why don't I just come over with some of that soup you like from The Font? It always helps you feel better. And I'm guessing you didn't eat much today." He would be correct, and also knows the way to my stomach is soup from my favorite restaurant on campus.

"Casey, I'm fine. In fact, I'm pulling up to the apartment now, and surprisingly, Trey is already here. So, if I need anything, he can get it for me. But you know I appreciate you, right?" I spot Trey's Jeep in the guest parking spot next to mine.

"That I do, James. That I do. All right, call me or text me later so I know you're okay." There's a slight edge to his voice, but then it softens. "Please."

I pull into my assigned parking spot in front of my apartment building and turn off my car. I tilt my head back onto the headrest and close my eyes to try to ease my headache. "Okay, I will. You should go out and have some fun with the guys tonight."

He laughs. "Yeah, okay. I might. Later."

"Bye." I open my eyes and press End on my phone.

Taking in a deep breath, I try to summon the strength to get out of my car and climb the one flight of stairs to my unit. My headache isn't lessening, and if I don't get some meds in me stat, I'm going to be in trouble. I grab my backpack from the passenger seat and get out.

On my way up the stairs, I hear loud music playing, but I can't tell where it's coming from until I reach the landing on my floor. It's definitely from my apartment, which doesn't make sense. I don't think that Trey would be blasting music while hanging out in my apartment. Maybe it's my roommate, Zoey.

As I'm putting my key in the lock, I hear Trey shout, but I can't make out what he's saying. When I push open the door, my body freezes, my eyes widen, and my jaw falls to the floor at what I see before me.

Trey is naked and pounding into my roommate, who is bent over the arm of the couch. They haven't noticed me yet, and I'm too stunned to say anything.

"That's right, Zo. Take my dick like a good little slut. I'm gonna wreck your fuckin' pussy." He grabs her hair and pulls it as he pistons into her, forcing her head back.

Zo?

When I move my gaze to her and look at her face, her eyes are closed, mouth open. She's clearly enjoying the wrecking of her pussy. It's carnal and raw. The kind of thing you'd see in a porno. Strange thing is … we have never, ever—in the two years we've been together, had sex like this.

I'm literally struck speechless.

"You feel so good, Trey. Fuck me harder," she moans out.

My bag slides off my shoulder and hits the ground. The sound makes them both look over at me.

And he. Keeps. Pumping.

"Oh shit. Fuck. Noelle!" Zoey screeches, and at least she has the decency to try to pull away from Trey and cover herself up with *my* blanket that's draped over the back of the couch.

He backs up, cock still hard—no condom—not bothering to cover his erection, and lifts his arms. "What the fuck, Noelle? Why are you home early?"

I can't seem to make my mouth move, both from the pain in my head and the scene before me. But when Zoey starts to walk over to me, I raise my arms out in front of me to stop her from getting anywhere close to me. "Do not come near me."

"I'm so sorry, Noelle. We didn't think you would be home so early." Not an *I'm sorry I'm fucking your boyfriend on our couch*, but *Sorry you came home early*.

I glance over to see Trey pulling up his boxers. The ones I bought him for Christmas this year that have little baseballs printed all over them. Un-fucking-believable.

"Right, well, I'm so sorry to interrupt. You two go ahead and enjoy yourselves." I pick up my backpack and turn to reach for the handle on the door as Trey takes a step forward.

"Noelle, wait. Fuck. This isn't what you think—"

"Oh, and, Trey, we're so fucking over." I boil with rage at Trey. "You need to be gone when I come back, and I never—I mean, *never*—want to see or hear from you again." I turn my attention to Zoey and point a finger at her. "And since my parents are paying for this apartment, you need to leave too."

"What?! Where am I going to go? We still have a few weeks left of school," she whines.

"Zo, I really don't care. Go stay with Trey!" I start to laugh, a little maniacal.

"Come on, Noelle. You're over—" he starts to speak, but I stop him.

"NO." Shaking my head and closing my eyes, I can't muster the strength to engage with him further. My head is full-on pounding now, and I need to get out of here. Fast.

When I open my eyes, I look at them both one last time. "Get the fuck out of my apartment by five p.m., or I'm calling the cops." I walk out the door, letting it slam behind me.

I rush down the stairs and get back into my car, throwing my backpack into the back seat. I know what I just saw, but also …

What the fuck just happened?

I never had any reason to suspect that they were messing around right under my nose—and in my own home, no less.

My hands are shaking, and my breathing is unsteady. I try pulling in some deep breaths to calm down, or at least clear my head enough so I can leave the parking lot without having to watch them leave.

Looking around my car, I search for my phone and realize I put it in the side pocket of my backpack when I got out earlier. I turn and reach for it, feeling it buzzing when I get ahold of it. I look at the screen and see it's Trey calling, and I immediately hit Decline. I can't hear his voice right now. And literally nothing he could say to me would erase what I just walked in on.

I'm so fucking stupid for staying with him as long as I did. I heard rumors that when we broke up, he would fool around with girls, and it hurt, but I convinced myself it was okay because we weren't together. But this I can't ignore.

There's only one person I want and *need* to see right now. The only person who could make this hurt less. I open my Recent calls and tap on his name, and it dials immediately.

"Well, that was—" he starts to say, but I interrupt.

"Casey, I need you." And then I start to cry.

CHAPTER
ONE

CASEY

PRESENT

IT'S QUITE possible my balls might just melt off today. The Oklahoma summer sun is no joke. I work a few days a week with Noelle at her father's marina on Lake Eufaula. The lake is just ten miles away from our hometown and about two hours from the Walker University campus. Even though I'm staying in our house on campus this summer, I come to the lake to be here for Noelle when I can. Especially because of what happened at the end of the year with her ex and roommate.

Trey, her ex, plays baseball on the Walker University team and is one of the biggest douchebags I've ever met. I tried several times to get her to break up with him, but for some reason, she was caught in his web. He was her first boyfriend, and he definitely played on her naivety and lack of relationship experience.

I know why he wanted her. It's the same reason I want her to be more than a friend. She's the most beautiful girl I've ever seen. But it's not just her looks; it's just *her*. She's the type of person who lights up the room with her smile, and she has one of the kindest hearts.

It's Fourth of July weekend, so the marina is busy. Boats are weaving in and out of the dock, and the convenience store is packed. Noelle works in the store while I help on the docks, filling gas and doing anything else her dad needs me to do.

When I pull into the employee parking area, I see her car and park next to it. As I'm pocketing my phone while I'm getting out of the car, it buzzes. I look at the screen and see it's Noelle texting.

Noelle: Are you almost here? We're getting pretty busy on the dock.

Instead of answering her, I walk into the store and see her behind the counter. There's a section that has supplies for boaters and fishermen, but the other side of the store has rows of snacks and food behind the counter, like hot dogs, burgers, nachos, and pretzels. Separating the food counter and the beverage coolers is a freezer that holds various ice creams and frozen treats.

She hasn't seen me yet, so I sneak around the back side of the checkout and stealthily come up behind her. I hold up my finger to my mouth to keep the person at the counter from reacting and alerting Noelle of my presence.

Stepping up to her, I put one hand on her hip and lean in to whisper in her ear, "You got any of them sausages cookin'?"

She jumps with a squeal and elbows me in the stomach. "Shit! Casey!"

She looks over her shoulder at me, but she's not mad. This is actually the first real smile I've seen on her in weeks.

Turning back to the customer, she finishes ringing up their order. "Your total for gas and the snacks will be one hundred fifty-three dollars and seventy-two cents."

He pays and walks away.

"Hang on, Casey. Let me get Duff to come over so I can show you where my dad wants you today." As she walks around me, her hand brushes my arm.

While I wait, I say hello to the next customer and spark up a conversation about the weather. Noelle and Duff—the teenage kid who works the early morning shift—come back over.

"Okay, King, let's roll." She grabs my hand, and we walk out of the store and down the dock toward the covered boathouse service area instead of the gas pumps. "My dad wants you to help my brother get all the kayaks and paddleboards set up along the shore for rentals. We couldn't get them out first thing because we had a line at the gas pump when we got here and we had to pull the Jet Skis out first too."

"Not a problem. Is Garrett in there now?"

"Yeah, he and my dad are pumping up the last two paddle-boards, last I saw." She drops my hand as we walk into the boathouse.

"Dad, Casey's here. Do you want him to start taking the kayaks out to the beach?"

"Hey, Case." He's bending down and sealing up the paddle-board, his back to us.

"Hey, Mr. James. Just tell me where you want me to start." I walk over to her brother, who is holding some of the oars, and give him a fist bump. "What's up, G-Man?"

Noelle's brother, Garrett, is in his junior year of high school. He's a good kid, pretty funny when you get him talking.

"Sup, Casey? You want to go start with that row, and we'll work our way down?" He nods to his right.

"You got it." I turn to Noelle and walk backward. "Are you staying out here or going back in?"

She laughs. "Oh, I'm definitely going back inside. It's way too hot out here. I might jump in later though once the rush dies down."

"Noelle, I'm not sure you're gonna get that break today. The lake is packed." Her dad stands and pulls the paddleboard over to the rest of the bunch that need to go outside.

"You're probably right. But I may jump in for a few minutes anyway."

"Come get me if you take a dip, and I'll come with," I shout as she walks out.

She looks at me and winks. It's playful, but not flirty, although I wouldn't mind if it was. She lifts her hand in a wave, and then I get started on the kayaks.

TWO

CASEY

A FEW HOURS LATER, I go back into the store, and it's slowed down a bit. There's a guy around our age standing at the counter, talking to Noelle. He's shirtless, in a swimsuit and no shoes. His back is burned, and there are clearly spots he missed with sunscreen. That's gonna hurt later.

As I walk up, it's obvious that he's flirting with her. And I can tell she's trying to be polite, but when she sees me walking toward her, she widens those big hazel eyes—so vulnerable and clear—and gives me a look that says, *I need you.*

I saunter up to her side as she lifts her arms to me and practically shouts, "There you are! Are we going swimming?"

I wink at her. "Yep, let's get out of here for a few and take a break." I nod to the guy at the counter. "Sup, man?"

He doesn't reply and turns and walks away.

"You came in at just the right time. I think he was going to ask me out, maybe, but I can't be sure. You know I'm not great at reading signals like that." She smiles awkwardly.

"Looked like you had it under control, but, yeah, he was

inching toward something." And it would have pissed me right off if he had asked for her number.

Thing is, yes, Noelle is my best friend. I would give anything to be more to her, but I'm too protective of our friendship to risk losing her by declaring my intentions and her not reciprocating. I'm surprised she didn't catch on a long time ago how I feel about her. For some reason, she can't see it or doesn't want to. I can't figure out which one it is. I mean, I think I'm a decent-looking guy, and I always try to make her feel important to me. Surely, she has to have some idea about my feelings for her.

"Hey, let's take the little boat out to the island for our break. It's been a while since we've done that." She grabs a set of keys under the counter.

"Lead the way." I hold my arm out and gesture for her to go ahead of me.

She reaches behind her, and I take her hand in mine. From an outsider's perspective, we might look like a couple because we have always been very affectionate in the sense that we hold hands and hug a lot.

We walk down the dock to the small boat tied near the end. Her hand still in mine, she steps into the boat and then releases my hand so I can untie the rope from the cleats.

Once I'm done, I toss the rope into the boat and hop in. Noelle has already started the engine, and we're slowly drifting away from the dock. We head toward the tiny island that's about two miles away from the marina by boat.

When we were in high school, we got lucky, drifting around the island one day, and found a patch that we claimed as Camp Coelle. It's been our place ever since. I've never seen anyone else use it. At least not when I'm here.

Noelle lowers the speed and drifts toward the shore. As we start to scrape sand, I go to the front of the boat, grab the rope, and hop out. I wrap it around a tree a few times, knot it, then walk back to the boat to help Noelle out.

As soon as her feet hit the sand, she toes off her shoes and drops them near the tree with the rope.

"I'm so hot. I can't wait to get in the water." She pulls her T-shirt over her head, and she's wearing a pink-and-white polka-dot bikini top under it.

When she starts to unbutton her shorts and pull them down, I wipe a palm over my mouth to make sure I'm not drooling. I'm trying not to be too obvious with my staring, but I can't help it. She's fucking gorgeous, and she doesn't even realize it.

I kick off my shoes, then pull my shirt off. I'm already wearing swim trunks, so I follow her into the water. We wade into the water until she's waist deep. When she stops, I face her as I walk backward, going deeper into the water, stopping when the water line is at my chest.

"Hey, not fair. I'm not as tall as you are." She pouts.

"You want me to come get you?" I start to swim back toward her.

"Yes, please. You can carry me." She holds her arms out as I get closer.

When I get to her, she wraps her arms around my neck, and I reach under the water and slide one arm under her knees and the other around her waist. I turn around and wade back into the deeper water, and she drops her head onto my shoulder. I know I shouldn't read into times like this, but they keep happening more and more since she and Trey broke up.

"You doing okay, pretty girl?" I rest my head on top of hers for a moment.

She nods, and her hair tickles my skin. "I'm good. Just tired. But, um, Trey was calling me again all morning, so I finally blocked him. At first, I'd thought he would take a hint. I mean, I think I was pretty clear when I broke up with him that we were over, but he won't let it go. I don't even really think he wants to be with me. I think he's just pissed that he can't have me and isn't controlling me anymore."

I'm really trying to stay calm here, but I'm over this fucking guy. I think she's right in a way. He's pissed that he doesn't have a say in her life anymore. But I'll keep my mouth shut and just listen because that's what she needs from me right now.

"You know I'm here for whatever you need. Trey is not my favorite topic, as you know, but I also don't want you to feel like you have to hide things from me if you need to talk."

She brings her hand up out of the water. "It's fine. And I know. I'm sorry I even brought it up. It's just really annoying. Anyway, enough about him. Are you staying for the fireworks?"

I nod, happy to change the subject. "Charlie and Beck are coming tonight to hang out. I told them we would meet them on the dock after we clocked out. I figured we could eat with them and watch the show. But if you're too tired, that's cool. I can take you back to your parents', and I'll come back and chill with them." I stop moving and sway us slowly in the water.

"Oh, that sounds fun. I'm sure I'll get a burst of energy at some point. I think I just need to eat a snack and have a Dr. Pepper. Anyone else coming with them?" she asks.

I shake my head even though she's not looking at me. "No, just them, as far as I know. Bo left for California yesterday for a week, and most of the other guys are home until the end of July."

"Are you getting excited to get back to football? Or are you dreading the workouts?" She lifts her head off my chest to look at me.

"I'm pretty excited to get back to it actually. It's not like I haven't been training, just not with the team. Beck and I work out every day, and I get my miles and sprints done in the morning. It's pretty quiet around there right now, so I've been running through campus." I start bobbing up and down in the water.

"I'm not really sure how I feel about going back. Like, I'm excited to get back to student teaching and going to your games, but I just feel so betrayed by my friends right now for not telling me that Trey was cheating on me with Zoey, so I'm dreading that part."

I kiss the top of her head before I lift her higher in the water because I'm gonna toss her. "You'll be just fine, pretty girl. You always have me, and Charlie wouldn't mind if you hung around with her and Arbor and Lily. You get along with them, don't you?"

"Yeah, I do. What are you doing?" She starts to squeal as I bounce us up and down. "Don't you dare dunk me, Casey King!"

"Noelle, I'm offended you would think I would stoop so low as to dunk you. I'm gonna toss you instead." I lift her out of the water and toss her a few feet away.

When she surfaces, I can't help but bust out laughing. Her hair is covering her face, and she looks … pissed at first. Once she swoops her hair out of her face, she gives me a pretty fierce staredown, which just makes me laugh harder. This girl doesn't have a mean bone in her body.

"It's not funny, Casey!" Although she starts laughing too. "I didn't want to get my hair wet before going back into the store."

"Oh, come on. I did you a favor. You were hot and sweaty. And no offense, but you were a little stinky, so I rinsed you off." I smirk.

She didn't smell. I just love to tease her.

"Excuse me, sir. I smell like roses at all times. How dare you!" She splashes me with water, which triggers a splash war.

I love it when we're like this together. She's been pretty messed up by the Trey situation, and I've done my best to try to make her happy again. Because she was never really happy with him. Sure, when they met, she was all about him, but the longer they were together, the more I saw her sparkle dim. It pissed me right off, and there were more than a few times I had to go over to her apartment and pick up the pieces. I fucking hate that guy.

"Okay, okay, I surrender!" she sputters. "We need to get back. Let's go, King." She starts walking out of the water to the beach.

I dive into the water and swim my way over to meet her. "Hey, did you bring any towels?"

"Oh, poop. No, sorry. We'll have to air-dry on our way back." She picks up her clothes and shoes and climbs back into the boat.

"I can help you get in the boat, you know?" I tell her.

"I know, but you need to untie it. And hustle so I can grab my DP before it gets busy again." She claps her hands.

"I'm comin'. I'm comin'." I untie the rope from the tree and push the boat off the sand. Once it's deep enough to start the engine, I lift myself into the boat.

When I'm in, I look up to see Noelle watching me, so I wink at her. Something I've noticed more lately is that she's been looking at me a little differently, watching me more maybe. Or it could be wishful thinking on my part.

She clears her throat, turns back to the wheel, and starts the engine. Because I'm a guy and like to do stupid things, I walk over to her and shake my hair right next to her. It would be easy for me to point out that she was checking me out, but I won't.

"Urgh! You're the worst!" She pushes me away from her with one hand, but laughs.

When we get back to the dock, I hop out again, tie up, and help her out of the boat.

Before we part ways, I reach for her hand to stop her. "Hey, please eat something. You can't survive on Dr. Pepper."

"I mean, I beg to differ. I could probably just hook it into an IV and walk around like that. DP running through my veins at all times." She wiggles her eyebrows and smiles.

"Noelle, I'm serious. Please eat something. I'm betting you haven't eaten yet today, and it's nearly two o'clock. It worries me when you do that, and I don't want you to get a migraine before tonight. I want you to watch the fireworks with us."

"You're sweet for caring, but I promise, I'm fine. I'll grab a snack when I get inside. Now, go do boaty things for my dad. I'll come get you when we're ready to shut down." She releases my hand and starts to walk toward the store.

"I'm gonna hold you to that promise!" I shout as I walk backward.

She doesn't have the best eating habits, and since Trey, it's only gotten worse. I need to keep her away from him this year. I need my sweet, happy friend back.

CHAPTER
THREE

NOELLE

CHARLIE AND BECK got here about an hour ago and have
been hanging out on the beach, waiting for Casey and me to
finish working. The sun is fading into night, which means fireworks will be starting soon. I need to finish cleaning up the store
for the morning shift, but first, I'll grab some food for all of us.
We don't have a wide variety at the store, but I did manage to
keep some of the barbeque sandwiches for us. They're Casey's
favorite.

The door opens, and Casey strolls in—shorts that sit low on
his hips, a tight white T-shirt clinging to his bronzed skin, and
dark hair that's perfectly tousled from drying in the sun after our
lake splashing. I can't lie and say I don't think Casey is hot. He
is. The way he held me today in the water not only made me feel
safe, but it was hard not to notice all that lean muscle I was
pressed against. And Lord knows I'm not the only girl who
notices. He's always had a flock of girls flirting and following
him around, but he is very selective.

I've heard rumors around campus, about him messing
around with girls, but he's not the kiss-and-tell type—at least not

with me. Trey always made sure to tell me when he saw Casey at parties with girls hanging around. I'm not sure why he made it a point to tell me. Probably to hurt me, which it did. I know I didn't have the right to feel the sting, but I just always think of Casey as mine. He's been my best friend for so long, and he knows me better than anyone, so I guess it feels weird for me to share him.

"Hey," he says, lifting his shirt to wipe his face, showcasing a sliver of his abs. "You ready to go? Charlie and Beck are waiting for us. Should we take the boat out to watch the fireworks?"

Clearing my throat and hopefully not drooling, I reach for the bag of sandwiches and snacks off the counter. "Yep, I'm ready. I got some food for us, but can you grab drinks out of the cooler? I don't plan to drink tonight since I'm driving the boat, but if you want to bring something for you guys, go ahead." I nod toward the direction of the cooler.

"Nah, I'm good. I need to head back to campus tonight."

"You aren't coming in tomorrow? I thought you had one more shift."

He walks up to me and throws an arm around my shoulders. "Sorry, pretty girl. Beck told me one of our teammates is moving in tomorrow and needs our help."

"Who is it?"

"It's a new guy. He's a cornerback transferring in from Georgia. Beck met him and says he's a decent guy."

Casey grabs a few drinks from the cooler and gets me a Dr. Pepper. Bless him. I walk over to the door and hold it open as he walks out. He reaches for the bag in my hand so I can get my keys out and lock the doors.

"Thanks, Case."

He winks at me and turns toward the dock. "Yo! Char! Come up to the dock. We're going to take the boat out."

I try to take the bag back from him, but he holds it out of my reach.

"I got it."

"I'm capable of carrying the bag, you know."

He looks at me and smiles. "I know you are, but I got it. Need to build up my muscles and get ready for training." He lifts the bag up and down.

"Right, right. So, the less than five-pound bag will really make a difference, I'm sure." I laugh.

"Hey, losers!" Charlie comes bouncing over to us. "Are we taking the boat out or what?"

Beck follows close behind, wearing a smirk as he watches his girlfriend jump on her brother's back.

"Char, get off! My hands are full." He tries to get her to slide off, but she doesn't.

She just laughs. "Awww, come on, little brother. You can't carry me? Not strong enough?"

"Seriously, bro. Get control of your girlfriend." Casey does a half spin to try to get her to fall off.

Beck just shakes his head.

"As if he would ever control me. Right, baby?" She jumps off Casey's back and moves to Beck and takes his hand.

"You're the boss, baby." He leans over and kisses the side of her head.

This. This is the way a relationship should look.

Trey never wanted to hold hands or show any kind of affection in public. It made me feel like he was embarrassed to be with me, but now I wonder if it was because he didn't want people to know he had a girlfriend so he could keep fucking around on me.

We reach the boat at the end of the dock, and Beck climbs in first and holds his hand out to Charlie to help her get in. Casey is next, and after he drops the bag and drinks, he holds his hand out to me, but I'm already halfway in.

"You want me to drive, or you got this?" Casey asks me.

"I'm good. I thought we would go around to the side of the island. We can see the fireworks better from there, and it's less crowded." I take the key out of my shorts pocket and start the engine.

After driving around the lake for a while, I get us to the side of the island. "Hey, Casey, can you grab the anchor? I think we'll drift too much if we don't drop the anchor."

"You got it." He stands from his seat and moves to the front of the boat, where the anchor sits.

Once he's lowered it into the water, I turn off the engine and make my way to the back of the boat. Charlie is curled up against Beck, her feet lying across the seat. They're both silently looking out over the water.

"You good?" Casey asks when he sits next to me and drapes his arm around my shoulders.

"I'm good. Ready for the show, you know?"

"Aha! That rhymes." Casey laughs, which makes me laugh.

A few minutes later, the first sparks light up the sky. It's a barrage of fireworks in blues, reds, and whites. A particularly loud firework shoots off, and it makes me jump. When I look at Casey, he's watching me.

"That was a loud one!" I scoot in closer to him.

He smiles at me softly. "I got you, pretty girl." Then he tucks a piece of my hair behind my ear.

His attention on me is making me feel … things. And as my gaze roams over his face and I see the fireworks reflecting in his eyes, I can't look away. Our faces are so close, in fact, that if I just leaned in a little, we would kiss—which would be crazy, right?

The thought startles me and snaps me out of my Casey haze, but my eyes are still on his. His thumb is brushing my shoulder softly, and if I didn't know better, I'd think he was looking at me in a more-than-a-friend kind of way.

CHAPTER
FOUR

PRACTICE STARTED TODAY, and my ass was cooked. I thought I had prepared and stayed in shape this summer, but the drills they had us running today nearly took me out. The heat didn't help. A few of my teammates even threw up on the field. *While they were running.* It was pretty gross, but not all that uncommon at the beginning of the season.

I'm sitting in the ice bath when my new roommate and teammate, Silas Arbuckle, walks over.

"Already in an ice bath, King? You a pussy or what?" He smirks.

"Fuck off, man. My legs feel like jelly. I need some recovery time. My body is a temple." I splash some water at him.

"Hey, yo! I don't need any of that. You coming back to the house after?"

"Yeah, I need some food and sleep."

"Do you want me to wait for you, or should I get a ride with Bo or Beck?"

He holds his fist out, and I tap it with mine.

"If they're ready, you can head back with either of them. I'm gonna soak for probably another ten minutes. I'll see you at home."

Beck walks up to us. "You need a ride, man?"

"Yeah, if you don't mind. King here needs a bath."

"Okay, let's roll. See you back at the house, Case." Beck bumps my fist with his, and they walk out.

Coach Pettys walks by next and stops and taps the side of the tub. "You feeling good, King?"

"All good, Coach. Ready for the season." I nod.

"That's what I need to hear. I'm counting on you this season. With Archie now in the pros, we've got a leadership gap. There's a lot of fresh talent coming in, and I need you and Linson to step up."

The look he's giving me tells me he's not fucking around. He's trusting us to set the tone, guide the younger guys, and hold the locker room together. And I know what he's really saying—if I don't lead, I could lose my starting spot. Talent alone won't keep me on the field this year. If he's handing me that kind of responsibility, then I need to prove I can carry it.

"Absolutely, Coach. You can count on me."

He lifts his chin, raises his eyebrows, and walks away.

Last season, I got my chance to start, and I'll do everything I can to make sure I keep my spot, but also become a key leader on this team.

When I walk into the house, I hear my roommates in the kitchen. Beck, Bo, and Silas are all standing around the small island we added to the kitchen this summer. We needed more counter space. Or at least that's what my sister said. And whatever Charlie says, Beck does.

"What's for dinner?" I ask when I walk in.

Beck looks over to me and nods. "Sup, man? We have some chicken on the grill. Charlie's out there now. Some veggies and taters too."

"Perfect. I'm starving." I grab a bottle of water out of the fridge and walk back to my bedroom. I drop my bag near my closet, then turn around and walk back to the kitchen.

My sister is walking in from the back porch with a plate in her hands that has several pieces of grilled chicken. "Can one of you go out and get the veggies and potatoes for me?"

Bo Callaway, our quarterback and one of my new roommates, starts walking toward the door before he responds, "You got it."

After last season and most of this summer, we've gotten to know him really well, and he has integrated into our group nicely. Despite the fact that his dad is a California Supreme Court judge and he comes from money, he's a really down-to-earth kind of guy.

When we lost our old roommates—quarterback Liam Pitz to Michigan and Archie Griffith got drafted to the pros—we wanted to be picky about who would be living with us this year. We aren't the party football house, and we needed roommates who followed along with our lifestyle. Bo easily clicked with us.

He's one of the most focused players I've ever seen. He's incredible to watch, and I'm pretty damn lucky to be on the receiving end of some of his talent. This guy is going to blow out all the existing records here at Walker, and he's only played one season. I'll be shocked if he stays all four years.

I'm still getting to know Silas, but he fits in pretty well. Keeps to himself a little, but I think as he gets to know us better, he'll loosen up a bit. Like me and Bo, he doesn't have a girlfriend—

that we know of anyway. He came to Walker to better his chances of getting drafted next year.

We all get food, then move to the table.

"Thanks, Char. I'm starving. This looks awesome."

One of the best benefits of having my twin live with us is that she's a damn good cook. She set a meal schedule for us last year, and we all took turns with family dinner nights, but she cooked more than any of us. She likes to take care of us. And with the exception of Beck, of course, the guys joke around with her and treat her like their sister too. Although when Liam and Archie lived in the house, they used to try to get a rise out of Beck by flirting with her when she first moved in and before they got back together, but again, they looked at her like a sister.

"We gonna make a new schedule for this year, or are you cooking all the family meals?"

She looks up at me with a glare, which only makes me smile. I don't expect her to, but like I said, she usually takes over. Especially when we were in playoffs.

"I'm sorry, Casey. Are your hands broken? Did you forget how to make food? I think not. Yes, a new schedule will be made."

Bo clears his throat. "Um, can I ask what family meals are? Like, y'all just have dinner together or what?"

"We sit together as a house one night each week, and we rotate the cooking duties," Beck answers before taking a larger than normal bite of chicken.

"Okay, cool, cool. Problem for me is … I don't know how to cook." Bo looks over at my sister and winces, then gives her a smile.

Now, I know my sister as well as I know myself, and while we have a lot of similarities, she's much … bossier than I am. She doesn't have nearly as much patience as I do either.

"Okay, silver spoon, we'll have to fix that real quick. Just because you're the superstar on campus doesn't mean you're getting out of pulling your weight in this house. Got it?" She's pointing her fork at him, but returns his smile.

Bo nods. "Totally get it. You just might have to tell me what to do. I can always look up videos, too, but I'm not great at picking food for other people. I can be pretty picky."

"Oh, Bo Callaway, I'm gonna have fun teaching you how to be a responsible big boy." She laughs.

"Shit," Beck mumbles and rolls his eyes.

Silas raises his hand. "Um, so I know how to make a few things, but you might have to teach me too."

"Oh, for fuck's sake. Are you both mama's boys or what?" She sets her fork on her plate and crosses her arms over her chest.

Beck and I both start laughing, knowing how much this is irritating her.

"Well, I mean I was the baby in the family." Silas shrugs.

She turns and looks at Bo.

"No matter what I say here, you'll probably tease me, so let's just go with, I didn't have the opportunity to learn. I can't help it that my parents had chefs and nutritionists for me."

"Okay, buddy." She shoots an okay gesture at him. "I'll be fixing that right away. Tomorrow, after practice, we'll start with some basics, like breakfast foods. In the meantime, we'll work on the calendar after we eat. We'll let Casey and Beck take the next few weeks, so I can teach you both a few things."

They both nod and smile at her. "Yes, ma'am."

"Case, when does Noelle get to campus? Did she find a new apartment yet?" Beck asks.

"She found a place and a new roommate. It's a girl she met in the dorms our freshman year. Wants to be a lawyer or something. I think they'll be a much better match than fuckin' Zoey. What a bitch." I shake my head.

"Ew. I can't even. I'm still flabbergasted by that whole thing. She's not still talking to him, is she?" my sister asks. "She seemed okay the last time we saw her."

"She's good, but I think she downplays how much she's hurt because she knows that I hate Trey. He never deserved her." I clench my jaw.

I seriously hate that guy. Not only because he hurt my best friend either. I know he was messing around on her probably the whole time they were together, but I never had any actual evidence, and when I would even allude to it, she would shut me down.

"What happened, and who's Noelle?" Silas asks.

Beck speaks up this time. "Noelle went to school with us back in Troy. She and Casey are attached at the hip. It borderlines on obsession. I'm sure you'll see her around here a lot. Even when she had a boyfriend, they were together all the time."

"Especially now. She came home to find her boyfriend fucking her roommate," my sister explains. "He's a total asshole. And not just because of the cheating. He thinks he's God's gift to women around here. He's on the Walker baseball team."

"Damn, that sucks. So, she's single now. Is she hot?"

"Hands off, Arbuckle," I warn, and he flinches.

"Wow. Okay. I see there's a bit more to the story. Girl's a perfect ten and clearly spoken for. You gonna make your move or what, King?" Silas asks.

I shake my head and look up to meet my sister's eyes. She knows the extent of my feelings for Noelle. I've told her everything. Not even Beck knows how far gone I am for this girl.

"I'm not sure it's worth ruining my friendship with her if she doesn't feel the same."

"That sucks, man. I'm sorry." Bo speaks up. "She's a nice girl."

"It's all good. I just want to be in her life, so however that looks is what I'll be." I give him a forced smile.

The conversation continues to discuss the upcoming season, but my mind is on Noelle.

CHAPTER
FIVE

NOELLE

THERE'S no doubt I got lucky getting an apartment this summer. Most places are secured at the end of the school year. I couldn't stay in the same complex I was in last year. Too many memories with Trey, and I don't think I could ever wash that visual from my mind when I walked into the apartment.

This complex is one of the newer ones off campus and fairly close to the school where I student teach. I'll be spending more time at the elementary school this year, so it actually worked out for the best. In all ways.

My parents pay for the apartment, but I like having a roommate who can split the utilities with me. As luck would have it, my friend Chelsea Sullivan—a girl I became friends with my freshman year—reached out to see if I knew anyone looking for a roommate. She had been living in the dorms last year, but didn't want to live in them this year. She's an awesome girl, very studious, and we've always gotten along well.

I back my car into my designated spot and see Chelsea waiting inside her car next to mine. She looks up and waves when she sees me. After putting the car in park and turning it off, I get out and walk around to meet her.

"It's good to see you. I'm so glad this worked out. I was low-key panicked about my living situation this year." She gives me a hug and squeezes me.

"Same! I was stressing about living alone, so you reaching out was perfect timing. Everything happens for a reason." I back away from our embrace and walk to the back of my car, where I have bins with my clothes and other personal items.

My dad and brother are following with a small trailer that holds my furniture. Casey and a few of his friends are supposed to meet us here and help get the big stuff moved in.

"Do you have stuff you need help with? My dad, brother, and my friends are coming to help with my furniture. They'll be more than happy to help." I open the trunk of my car.

"That would be awesome. My aunt and sister should be here any minute with my big stuff. I don't have much since you had the couch and most of the furniture already, but I do have a bed that we could use some help with," she says as she opens her own trunk.

We both grab a few things, close our trunks, and walk toward the building. We're on the first floor, which isn't ideal for safety reasons, but it was the best we could do. And today, in this heat, I can't say that I mind not having to walk up and down the stairs.

I picked up the keys a few days ago when I came to campus to buy supplies for my classes this semester. When we reach the door, I set my bag and the small bin I was carrying on the ground and reach into my pocket for my keys. After I unlock the door, Chelsea walks in first, and I lift my things and follow.

The layout is a little different from my apartment last year, but I like it much better. The living area is open, and there's a tiny kitchen toward the back of the space, but it opens to the living room. Looking to the left, I see the small patio that could probably hold a round table and maybe two chairs. Turning right from the door is the hallway that leads to the two bedrooms and a hall bathroom. I have a bathroom in my room as well.

"This is really great, Noelle. It's the perfect size for us." Chelsea walks over to the kitchen area and sets a bag on the counter.

"Yeah, I don't love living on the ground floor, but we'll take what we can get, right?" I shrug, then set down my bag and bin. I walk into the kitchen and take a look in the fridge to make sure we don't have any surprises to clean out.

"Literally anything is better than living in the dorms this year. I really don't think I could handle it again. The smell in the hallway alone was brutal." She laughs.

"I don't miss the dorms at all, but we did have fun our freshman year." I smile at her.

"Oh, for sure. It was a lot of fun. I don't really talk to anyone other than you anymore though. Do you?" she asks.

"Not really. Zoey was my roommate last year, but you know how that ended. And some of the other girls we became friends with … I just can't talk to them right now, you know?" I walk out of the kitchen and toward the hall. "Come on. I'll show you to your bedroom."

She follows, and when we reach her doorway, I step to the side and let her go into the room first.

"This is perfect and honestly a little bigger than I thought it would be."

"Yeah, they're decent-sized rooms. I like that this building is newer too. Our apartment last year was older, and it seemed like something always needed to be repaired. When we moved in last fall, it was disgusting. It took us, like, two days to clean it."

"That's gross. No, this is nice and clean. My bathroom is across the hall?" She starts to walk toward me in the doorway, so I back away and she walks around me to the bathroom across from us. "This is great. Again, thank you for letting me be your roomie." She reaches for my hand and squeezes it.

"Of course. I'm really glad this worked out." My cell phone buzzes in my back pocket, and I pull it out to see my dad texting to tell me they're outside. He hasn't been here yet, so he's not sure which unit is mine. "My dad and brother are here, so I'm going to go help them."

"Okay, I'll come out in a few. I'm just going to use the bathroom first." She walks over to the counter and grabs her bag off it.

"Meet you out there." I open the door and see my dad getting out of the truck and walking to the back of the trailer. I don't see my brother, so he must be back there already.

As I'm walking to meet them, I see Casey's truck pulling into the complex with Beck's truck behind his. I lift my arm to wave him over. They both pull in across from where my dad is parked.

Charlie hops out of Beck's truck first. "Hey, chick! How's the place?"

We meet halfway and hug. Last year, when she came to Walker, we spent more time together since Casey and I are together quite a bit, and she and I have become closer.

"It's good. I'm dreading this part though. I feel like it takes me forever to unpack."

"I'll help you, and we'll get it done fast," Charlie says.

Beck walks over to us and hugs me. "Hey. Good to see you. Where do you want us to start?"

The "good to see you" makes me smile. Beck isn't really talkative, but when he does speak, you know he means what he's saying.

"Hey, Beck. Thanks for coming to help. I appreciate it." I smile. "We might as well get started with the big stuff so my dad and brother can head back home. They have to return the trailer by five p.m."

Casey, Bo Callaway, and a new guy walk over to join us.

"Hello, Noelle James. It's good to see you on this fine Oklahoma day," Casey says, walking over and wrapping me into a hug.

A thought hits me that Trey and his friends would have never come by, let alone offered to help me move. I don't know how I didn't pick up on those red flags.

Yet here are some of Walker football's starting lineup, ready to help me.

"Hello, Casey King. It's good to see you as well." I pull back and slap his stomach. "You're a nerd."

We both smile and laugh.

Bo nods at me. "Hey, Noelle."

I don't know him as well, we aren't at the hugging stage yet, so I just lift my hand and smile.

The new guy reaches out his hand toward me. "Hey. I'm Silas."

"Hey, Silas. You're the one from Georgia?" I ask him.

"That would be me. I came from playing for Georgia, but I'm from Arkansas."

We shake hands, and he pulls his hand away.

"Gotcha. So, you're closer to home now. Welcome to Oklahoma!"

"Okay, James, let's roll. I'm hungry, and I want to get this done before it gets hotter." Casey starts walking toward my dad and brother, and the guys follow.

Chelsea walks over, and I introduce her to Charlie. Then we walk over to the guys and my dad and brother.

"I feel like you guys have control of this situation, so we'll start taking stuff out of my car." I lift my thumb over my shoulder.

"We need to bring in the furniture first so that the boxes or whatever you have aren't in the way, so let us get this stuff in first. Won't take us long since I have some of the stars of Walker here to help us." My dad laughs.

"Oh, right. I guess that makes more sense. So, what do you want us girls to do?" I ask.

"Just look pretty and tell us where to go," Casey chirps.

"I like that answer," Charlie says.

"Just show us where everything goes, and once we're done with that, we'll get your cars cleared out," Dad says. "Hi, I'm Noelle's dad, Brad." He holds out his hand to Chelsea.

"Hi, Mr. James. I'm Chelsea. I think we met a few times during my freshman year." She shakes his hand.

"Oh, right! Your hair is different?" he asks.

Chelsea laughs. "Yes! I was in a hair coloring phase, and I think it was either pink or purple the last time I saw you."

Dad snaps his fingers. "That's what it is! Good to see you again then. I'm glad you girls could work this out." He turns and walks to the back of the trailer.

"Chelsea, let me introduce you to everyone." I grab her hand and pull her over to me. "You probably remember Casey."

"Yep, I do. Hi, Casey." She nods.

"Hey, Chelsea. Good to see you." He smiles at her.

"This is Beckham, who is Charlie's boyfriend and Casey's best friend. We all grew up together too. This is Bo Callaway and Silas … I don't know his last name." I laugh.

"Arbuckle. Like the mountains," he says, giving a crooked grin and placing his hand on his chest.

"Hey, y'all. Good to meet you." She waves her hand and smiles.

I'm glad she's not shy because this group can be intimidating if you don't know them. Just from their size alone.

Casey claps his hands together. "Let's do this. I'm sweating my nuts off out here already."

With these guys here, along with Charlie and Chelsea, it feels like I'm starting off the year right. I just need to stay focused on school and spend time with people who really care about me. Fuck Trey.

CHAPTER
SIX

NOELLE

EVERYTHING HAS BEEN amazing since we moved into our new apartment. Chelsea and I are very similar in our routines, so it's been easy to get into a flow with school. My course load is heavy this semester, so having a roommate who cares about school as much as I do is really nice.

I'm on my way to my second class of the day, but I desperately need a coffee and have a few extra minutes to swing into the food court. As I pull the door open, I bump into a really tall guy with a very hard chest. When I lift my head, I meet Trey's eyes.

"Noelle. I've been trying to get ahold of you, so this is perfect." He grips my arm.

"Let go, Trey." I try pulling my arm out of his grasp.

"Baby, come on. Don't be like this. I said I was sorry." He squeezes my arm a little tighter.

Trey is six feet five inches, which he likes to use to intimidate people. I'm no match for him in size or strength.

"Trey, if you don't let go of my arm, I will scream." My heart is starting to pound in my chest, and I feel the onset of a panic attack coming.

He drops my arm and holds his hands out. "Jesus, Noelle. Drama much? I just want to talk to you."

"I have nothing to say to you. In fact, I would be so happy to never see or talk to you again. Now, get out of my way."

I can feel my hands starting to shake and try to walk around him, but he blocks me.

He lifts his hand, and with his index finger, he tilts my chin to meet his gaze. "It was a mistake. You need to get over it. You know how I feel about you, baby. Why don't you let me come over and we can talk about it?"

I grab hold of his wrist and pull his hand away from my face. "Don't ever touch me again."

When I move to walk around him this time, he lets me pass.

"Noelle. You're being ridiculous about this. Come on, baby." He huffs.

I don't turn around as I'm walking, but I do lift my middle finger over my shoulder. He laughs as I keep going, but … I'm still shaking.

It's been three days since my run-in with Trey, and he hasn't left me alone since. I'm not sure if he somehow found out my class schedule or what, but every time I walk out of class, he's there. He hasn't tried to touch me again, and he really doesn't even say much, but he's there.

When he does speak to me, it's as if nothing happened at all. Of course, I don't reply, but it doesn't stop him.

Today, he brought me a bouquet of roses, which I refused. I really just want him to leave me alone.

My move, my new roommate situation, and school were starting off so well until I saw him.

My last class of the day has ended, and I'm trying to figure out the back way out of the building to avoid seeing him, if he's waiting for me again. When I reach the end of the hallway, I look to my left and see a door that doesn't say *Fire Escape*, so I walk over and push the door open, thankful that an alarm doesn't start blaring.

There's no sign of Trey, but I have to walk around the building and through the courtyard to get to the parking lot where I parked my car today. I glance around me to see if I can see him, but I don't, so I slow my pace. I pull out my phone to check my texts. I felt it buzz a few times while I was in class. There's a text from Casey.

Casey: You coming over for dinner tonight?

Noelle: Sorry, I was in class. Yes, I think so.

Casey: Chelsea can come, too, if she wants. We'll have plenty of food.

Noelle: Who's cooking tonight?

Casey: Moi.

Noelle: So … we're having spaghetti?

Casey: Funny. No, we're not actually. It's not a carb load day, so we're having tacos.

Noelle: Yum. Chicken or beef?

Casey: I made both.

Noelle: Do you need me to bring anything?

Casey: We're all set, pretty girl. See you later.

I like his message and put my phone into my back pocket.

"There you are!" Trey's hand grabs my elbow.

"Let go, Trey." I pull my arm out of his hold and start walking quickly again.

He's walking next to me, and he has a smile on his face. Like he thinks this is funny. "Noelle, Noelle, Noelle. When will you get it in that head of yours that you're mine? I love you, baby. What you and I had was awesome, and I fucked it up. I hate myself. You're killing me with how you keep running away from me."

I stop walking and turn to face him. This sweet-talking. The sincerity in his tone. The way his mouth quirks to the side in a lopsided grin that's almost childlike. It's endearing, and it eats away at my heart.

"Trey, you hurt me. I cried for weeks. You cheated on me and looked me in the eye while you fucked my roommate."

"I know you were upset, and I get it, but that was months ago. You need to get over it. Zoey was just a fuck buddy."

My brows curve as I tilt my head and step back. "Get over it?" I blanch at his words. I've known all summer what a fool I was to be with him, but now that realization is cemented in my heart. "Oh, I'm over it. But you won't leave this alone. No, I'm not going to listen to you tell me how much you love me and how much you hated what you did. It's not worth my time. You're harassing me at this point, and it has to stop. I'm not falling for your lies anymore. I've blocked you from my phone, and yet you've somehow found out my class schedule and wait for me after class. It's got to stop. When are *you* gonna get that into that head of *yours*?" I'm practically yelling now.

He looks around, clearly not liking the vocal rejection in the middle of campus. His sweet demeanor changes to a cocky bravado. "Why would I need to stalk you? I can literally have any girl on this campus. If you knew what you were doing in bed, I wouldn't have had to hook up with Zoey to begin with," he snaps in my face, and it makes me flinch.

"The world is your oyster then, I guess. Have at it. All the ladies. Besides, I have a boyfriend. One who loves me, respects me, and wants to take care of me."

The words barely leave my mouth before I wish I could pull them back.

Because when I said it, it wasn't him I saw.

It was Casey.

Because I am having a complete moment of word vomit, I add, "Who I am having wild, crazy, raunchy sex with—and not just the missionary kind!"

"The fuck, Noelle? Who the fuck are you with? There's no way. I don't believe you. Who? Tell me." His hands are on his hips, and his face is turning red.

I swallow and try to get control of my voice before I answer, "Casey."

"King! Motherfucker. I told you he had a thing for you! Were you messing around with him the whole time we were together? That's what all those sleepovers, dinners, and bullshit were then? You fucking around on *me*?" He moves his hands from his hips and pulls the baseball hat off his head and runs one hand through his hair, pulling it.

"You can't be serious. You know I was always loyal to you. Don't you dare try to turn this on me. You were the cheater, Trey. You! Now leave me the fuck alone!"

I start to walk away, but he grabs my arm again, this time squeezing hard, his fingers digging into my skin.

He pulls me closer despite my resistance. "Okay. Okay, baby. You go have your fun with King, but you'll come running back to me. You always do. You're nothing without me, and you know it." Now he tries the tactic that used to work on me, making me believe I was worthless or stupid.

"That's where you're wrong. I'm more than enough without you and everything to him." As I'm saying the words, I know I might be fabricating our relationship, but the words … they're true.

Trey releases my arm and shoves me away from him. "Fine, okay. I get it. This is your payback. But I'll be waiting. Because I meant what I said. You're mine."

"Hey, Noelle."

I turn toward the deep voice saying my name to see Silas standing there.

"You good?" He looks at Trey, jaw clenched, fists tight.

"Oh, hey, Silas. I'm fine." I start to walk toward him, but glance back at Trey. He's wearing a sinister smile.

"Bye, Noelle. I'll see you soon," he says, then turns and walks away.

"Who is that guy?" Silas asks.

"My ex," I say, shaking my head.

"The one who cheated?" He tilts his head back and shuts his eyes. "Shit. Sorry."

I huff a laugh. "No, it's okay. Yes, he's the cheater." We both start walking. "I'm good. If you have somewhere you need to be, you don't have to hang around on my behalf."

"I'm heading this way. I have an Econ class next. I'll walk with you till I need to split off, if that's cool." He tilts his head, assessing me. "Besides, you know what fine stands for?"

"Uh, that I'm okay?" I shrug.

"Fucked up, insecure, neurotic, and emotional. So, tell me again, are you *fine*?" He studies me again.

"Yeah, of course." A thought runs through my mind, and butterflies flutter in my belly. "So, um, how much of our conversation did you hear?" It's not that I care if he heard it necessarily; I just want to be the one to talk to Casey about it first.

"What do you mean?" he asks, adjusting the strap of his backpack on his shoulder, looking slightly awkward, which tells me he must have heard something.

"Silas, you and I are probably going to be around each other a lot, so let's just … get it out there. What did you hear?" I say as I mindlessly wave my hand in a circle. I tend to use my hands when I'm feeling nervous or insecure.

Silas stops walking and turns to look at me. "Look, I have no idea what's going on, and it's really none of my business. Whatever is happening with you and your ex … well, if he's bothering you, you should tell someone. And I'm betting Casey would want to know about it—you know what I mean? As far as anything else I heard, that's between you and Casey." He gives me a sympathetic smile. "But word to the wise: you'd better tell him before he hears it from someone else. And for the record, that someone won't be me. You seem like a nice girl, and if my roommates are tight with you, that means I will be too. Family, on and off the field, is important to me."

I nod. "Oh, yeah. I will talk to him about it tonight. I haven't said anything about Trey following me around yet though because I knew Casey would be upset about it and I was handling it my way. But, uh, thanks again for interrupting us. It was heading in a direction I didn't want to go." We start walking again. "You going to be at the house tonight for dinner?"

"Hell yeah. King said he's making tacos. That's one of my favorites." He claps his hands together and smiles. "I need to head this way." Silas leans his head to the right. "You good to get to your car?"

I place my hand on his forearm. "Yeah, I'm good. Thanks again, Silas. See you tonight." My hand drops, and I give a slight wave goodbye.

He lifts his chin and walks away. As I start walking again, I can't help but look around for Trey. After what was said today and the fact that he's been obviously following me around, I know I should have made a break from him a long time ago, but I can't go back and fix it. But I do need to get to Casey before Trey starts asking around about us.

Knowing Casey the way I do, I don't think he'll be mad about what I said. However, he'll want to drive over to the baseball house, where Trey lives and … well, I don't know what Casey would do. He's never shown any violence or volatility like Trey has, but he is really protective of everyone he cares about.

And even though it's a big campus, rumors around the athletic world circulate fast, and I just hope he will play along with the whole boyfriend thing. Guess I'll find out tonight.

CHAPTER
SEVEN

CASEY

TONIGHT WAS my night to cook, and after my sister told me a few of her friends were coming over, too, I decided to go with something that was easy to make for a lot of people. So, tacos it is. I'll have a deconstructed taco though because I have to count my carbs, and I'll eat grilled chicken in mine, which is pretty plain, to keep my sodium on the lower side so I don't cramp up during practice.

I hear the front door open and girls' voices. My sister and her friends, Arbor and Lily, walk into the kitchen. We grew up with Arbor. Her mom and mine were best friends here at Walker, so I've known her my whole life. I've gotten to know Lily better over the past year since Charlie moved in with us. Arbor is like a sister, but Lily is … not. She's been dating some frat guy, but she still flirts with all of us—except for Beck, of course. They've both become good friends for my sister, and I'm glad she's found her people.

"Be right back. I'm going to see what Beck's up to." Charlie starts to walk away. "Hi, brother! Smells awesome in here."

"Charlie, dinner starts in ten minutes, with or without you and Beck," I yell after her.

"Sup, Casey?" Arbor says, opening the fridge to put some of the fancy sparkling water drinks she likes in there.

"Arbs. Lily. How's it going?" I smile at them both while I sort cheese, lettuce, salsa, and sour cream in some bowls.

"Well, Casey, since you asked, it's going pretty amazing. I had a fab time in Italy this summer with my boyfriend's family, and now we're talking about moving in together for senior year. He has to live in the frat this year because he's the president." Lily leans her hip against the counter next to me while she rambles on. "Oh, is that fresh salsa?" She doesn't wait for me to reply and walks over and starts digging into the chips and salsa.

"That's awesome. Good for you." I shoot her a wink. "How 'bout you, Arbs?"

"Case, I saw you, like, a ton this summer. But classes are good so far." She walks over to me and looks around me to see what I'm doing. "Yum. I'm so excited for tacos. It's my love language. Do we have any guac?"

"Shit, I forgot to slice the avocado. Can you grab it for me and the onion and tomato?" I reach below me and pull the cutting board out of the cabinet in front of my legs.

"Yep. You have lime too, right?" She bends and peeks inside the drawer in the fridge.

"Should be in there." I nod.

"Found it!" Arbor sets everything on the counter next to me.

"Thanks. Do you want to slice the lime for me? You know I'm not the best at it since I sliced my finger in middle school. I still have nightmares from that sting." I hand her a knife and give her a smirk.

She starts to laugh and hip-checks me. "You're such a baby, Case. Didn't some of the juice get in your eye, too, and you couldn't see for, like, three hours?"

We both start laughing, and then I wrap my arm around her shoulders, pulling her into me. "Don't make fun, Arbs. That was traumatic for me. And you and Charlie just teased me all day about it."

"I mean, how could we not? And you have to admit, the homemade eye patches were top-tier. You looked just like Jack Sparrow." She wraps her arm around my waist and looks up at me, and we both laugh.

I hear a throat clear and look over Arbor's head to see Noelle standing there in leggings and a long-sleeved shirt, next to the island, holding a dish. I can't quite read the look on her face, which is unusual because I've memorized all her faces.

"Hey! You made it." I drop my arm from Arbor's shoulders and walk over to her. "You okay?"

"Hey!" she squeaks. "Hi, Arbor." She places the dish on the island counter and walks over to Arbor and hugs her.

"Hey, lovely. How are you? I haven't seen you since the end of the year. I'm glad you came tonight." Arbor gives her a warm smile.

If Arbor doesn't like you, you know it. My sister's friends have gotten to know Noelle a little last year, and they all seem to get along well. She really needs some friends, so I'm glad she's getting to know them better.

"I'm good-ish." She laughs nervously. "Hectic start to the year, getting used to my class schedule and student teaching. How about you? Are you in the house again this year?"

"Yeah, I'm going to stay one more year, I think. We'll see what happens."

"Hey, Noelle," Lily says with a mouthful.

Noelle walks over to her and gives her a side hug. "Hey, hey. How's your man?"

"Dreamy." Lily closes her eyes and smiles.

"That's awesome, Lily. So happy for you."

Noelle forces a smile, but I'm the only one who sees her pained expression. Something is definitely going on, and I'm about to ditch this dinner to find out what it is.

She walks over to me and notices me watching her. "What?"

I place a hand on her shoulder. "You okay?"

"Mmhmm. I'm good. I brought some cookies for dessert. I know you guys have to watch what you eat, but a few won't hurt, right?" She smiles at me.

"Chocolate chip?" I raise an eyebrow and smirk.

"Your favorite."

This time, I get a real smile. She reaches over me to grab some shredded cheese from the bowl. When I look down, I see a bruise on her forearm. Clearly fingerprints.

What the fuck?

I reach out and gently take her arm in my hand. "Noelle. Who did this to you?" I look at her face to see her eyes. My stomach tightens, and I feel sick to my stomach.

"Case, it's fine. I'm fine. I promise. We'll talk later, okay?" She removes my hand from her arm and pulls the arm of her long-sleeved shirt down to her wrist.

The fact that she is wearing a long-sleeved shirt in this heat didn't exactly register with me because we keep our house cold and she's always cold. But I think this time is because of the bruise. It's still hotter than hell outside.

"Who hurt you?"

Her eyes shift, and she gives me a reassuring smile. "Not here, okay? I promise I'm totally good, and I will tell you the whole story later."

"Stay after dinner." My tone is commanding, and I can feel the shift in her energy as she takes in a deep breath.

If I push too hard, Noelle will act like whatever is bothering her, whatever happened, never did. She'll shut me out because that's what she does to protect herself from dealing with hard situations.

I change my tone. "We can watch a movie, or do you need to get home early tonight?"

She nods. "I think I can hang around for a while."

"Perfect." I relax, knowing she's not going anywhere. "Okay, let's get everyone in here to eat. I'm starving." I clap my hands together. "It's taco time!" I yell.

The sooner I can get this dinner over with, the better. I want some time with my girl.

I feel like I inhaled my dinner tonight. Noelle seemed fine with everyone at dinner, although she didn't eat much. But that's not uncommon when something's on her mind.

Walking into my room after stopping in the bathroom to brush my teeth, I see her lying on my bed, propped against the headboard. Long legs, arms crossed over her chest, and her fingers playing with her full lower lip—a thing she does when she's overthinking … which she does a lot. She's been in my bed like this more times than I can count. Like she owns the place—and part of me—and doesn't even know it. But now that I know Trey is out of the picture, this is like a goddamn fantasy. The amount of control I have right now? I should get a fucking medal for not physically showing off how my body reacts to the sight of her.

"What're we watching, pretty girl?" I walk over to the bed and drop onto my back.

Her laugh is light, but there's also a bit of nervousness to it. "Uh, I don't really care what we watch, but there's something I need to talk to you about."

I knew it. "Okay, yeah. What's going on? You okay?" I reach over and take her hand. There's a slight tremble to it, so I run my thumb over the top, trying to calm her.

"Yes." She shrugs.

"Okay … you gonna tell me?" I smile at her.

She takes a deep breath in. "Before you completely freak out, let me tell you everything first, okay?"

Well, fuck. That doesn't sound good. And I swear to God, if she's about to tell me she's getting back with Trey … I'm gonna have to walk out of the room. Instead of answering with words, I just nod.

"So, I ran into Trey recently. You know I'd blocked him after everything happened, and he wouldn't stop calling and texting, so I hadn't talked to him since that day we shall not discuss." She pauses and looks at my expression, which I'm keeping neutral. She continues, "I knew, coming back to campus, there would be times I might run into him, but not one-on-one, right?" She starts moving her hands, twisting her fingers around each other.

I nod. "Okay, and?"

"Well, he must have found out or figured out my schedule because, the last few days, he's been waiting outside my classes and following me around. He brought me flowers." She holds up her hand. "Which I didn't accept."

I'm a pretty calm guy by nature, but this guy makes me want to crash out. My jaw is clenched, to the point that I wouldn't be surprised if I cracked a tooth. And I can't lie and say we've never had a confrontation. Noelle just doesn't know about it.

She pauses, eyes roaming over my face. "I had it under control … until today. He told me he loved me and that everything was behind us. He told me to get over it and started spouting off about how I was his, and just in general, he was being an asshole. Why on earth I stayed with him, I have no idea." She looks down and shakes her head.

I mean, I know why she stayed with him. The guy's a narcissist and played into her emotions, but that's not what she needs to hear right now. She needs me to listen, so that's what I'll do.

"So, how did you get him to walk away?"

"Funny enough, Silas walked up to us. He must have recognized me from moving day and stopped. There was no hiding the fact that Trey and I were fighting, and I think he wanted to make sure I was okay." She tries to smile, and she reaches out and sets her other hand on top of mine.

I clear my throat. "And the bruise is from him?" I'm trying to stay calm, but I'm about to fucking lose it.

"Yes, He squeezed my arm pretty tight." I start to shift, but she squeezes my hand, trying to keep me in place. "Case, I'm fine. Honestly. I pissed him off, and that was his reaction. I just spoke before I thought about it."

"Noelle, no man should ever, for any reason, lay a hand on you. Do you hear me? Ever. You understand he needs to pay for this, right?" I shake my head back and forth.

"I know, and I agree. I'm not making excuses for him anymore, like I did when we were together." She tries to bring my attention back to her.

"I know of one other time he did something like this to you. Are you telling me it happened more than that?" I roll my lips over my teeth to keep from saying anything more. Like what I did to him when I found out about it for the first time.

"I mean, no. But honestly, Casey, I'm trying to tell you more about why he did it. Because it involves you. Something I said about you." She closes her eyes and tilts her head up. "Please don't be upset."

I sit up now because I can't imagine what would make me upset with her, aside from wishing she'd kicked him in the balls. "Tell me."

She lowers her head, opens her eyes, and looks at me. I can see pink tinting her cheeks, and she's holding her bottom lip between her teeth. "I'm not sure I can look at you when I tell you this."

I can't help but laugh because this girl is never shy with me. "Noelle, come on. Tell me what you said."

She covers her face with her hands. "I told him you were my boyfriend now."

My stomach drops, but not in a bad way. In a very fucking good way.

To make sure I heard her correctly, I pull her hands from her face and wait for her to open her eyes to look at me. "You told him I was your boyfriend?"

"And I might have alluded to us having sex. I believe my exact words were *wild, crazy … raunchy.*" She scrunches her eyes at the last word as if she's embarrassed. One of her eyes opens to gauge my reaction.

I'm not really sure how to react here. Internally, I couldn't fucking be happier. But I'm also not sure I want to show all my cards until I understand the situation fully.

"I'm sorry." She winces. "It just slipped out. He was going on about how I was his and how him cheating was my fault," she mutters. "I hope you're not mad. It just literally spilled out of my mouth. I don't want him thinking it's okay for him to keep following me around." Her head drops, and her hair covers her face, slightly hiding her from me.

"And I think I said you were my boyfriend because it was an easy answer and it was reactive because I knew our friendship always bothered him. Once I said it, I knew it was wrong because he's going to expect us to be a couple."

I don't think I could stop the smile from forming on my face if I tried. "I accept."

She laughs. "You accept?"

"You bet your ass I accept. You told him I'm your boyfriend because Trey is a manipulative motherfucker. Anything I can do to make him squirm, I'm game. What do you need from me then?"

"Casey, I thought you would be mad. Or feel weird about this." She tilts her head in question.

"Why would I feel weird? Definitely not mad." I laugh.

Her mouth is open in surprise. "I don't know. I mean, we

never really talk about your dating life, and I don't want to cramp your style or anything. I saw you and Arbor when I came in tonight. If you're interested in her or something, I don't want to ruin that for you. She's really pretty and so sweet."

I bark out a laugh and jump off the bed now. "Arbor? Arbor, as in the girl Charlie and I grew up with and who I think of as a sister? Yeah, love the girl, but not a single thought about her goes in that direction."

Noelle's face turns pink again, and she gives me a crooked smile. "Oh, okay, well you never know. You've known me for years. Like a sister—"

"I definitely do not think of you as a sister. You and I are … different. And as far as other girls … don't even think about it. For as long as you need me to be your boyfriend, I'm yours." I sit back down on the bed and take her hands in mine. "But I feel like I need to do this all official-like, you know?"

A smile breaks across her face. "Official?"

"Yeah, I mean, we have to have our story straight, right?"

Am I gonna milk this for all I can? You bet your ass I am.

I drop down on my knees, open my arms, and make a big show of my proposal. "Noelle James, will you be my fake girlfriend?"

"Casey King, I would be honored to be your fake girlfriend."

She giggles, then shoves me over with her foot. On my way down, I grab her by the hip and pull her on top of me, rolling her over beneath me. My hands run up her sides, and I start tickling her without mercy.

Her laugh—it's the sweetest music I've ever heard.

When she showed up tonight, it was with a frown and that invisible wall she always keeps up. But now, in my arms, wriggling and squealing with laughter, she's completely alive. Trying to escape yet loving every second of it. I admire the beauty beneath me, at the way I'm the one who put that smile on her face.

"Okay, so that went better than I'd expected it to," she says as she catches her breath, her hair spilled across the carpet and her hand on her chest. "I thought you might be irritated that I threw that out like that."

I roll my head to look at her. "Irritated? Yeah, no. Am I pissed that that fucker is following you around? Yep. Am I gonna do something about it? Also yep." I huff a laugh.

"Casey, no. Leave it alone. You aren't risking your position on the team for this." She shakes her head.

"Nah, I won't. I promise. But for the foreseeable future, I'll be walking you to and from classes as much as I can. And if I can't, I'll make sure someone else can."

"You don't have to go above and beyond."

I lift up on my elbow and peer down at her. "Hell yeah, I will. If you're my girl, then you're getting the full Casey King treatment."

I mean, this is gonna be fun. I'm gonna ride it for as long as it takes to make her see that this can be real.

CHAPTER
EIGHT

TRUE TO HIS WORD, Casey has walked me to and from class as much as he can. And I've only seen Trey from a distance. I can't say he's following me or if he just happens to be in the same place at the same time. Still suspect. If Casey can't be with me, one of the guys from the team or his sister and her friends— or I guess my friends too—meet me. I hate interrupting their schedules, but Casey won't accept anything else right now with Trey still lingering around.

He runs my class pickup schedule the way Charlie keeps the weekly cooking calendar. Apparently, the Kings like to make lists.

As far as the amount of time we're spending together ... yeah, it's more than usual. And that's saying something because we've always been around each other. But now it's different. I notice things—how his eyes crinkle when he smiles, how he always remembers the smallest details, like the way I take my tea or the fact that I hate Tuesdays. I used to think of him as just my best friend. Safe, familiar. But lately ... he feels like more. And I think—no, I *know*—I like it. The problem is, I know it's fake. He's putting on a show in case Trey or one of his baseball buddies sees us around—which they have, and I'm sure they're reporting back. It seems to be working because Trey has left me alone.

Tomorrow is Casey's first football game, so we're staying in tonight. It's an early game, so he needs to chill as much as possible and definitely get a good night's sleep.

Charlie and I made dinner together for the guys. We made salad and pasta, and there wasn't a noodle left. I thought Archie and Liam could eat a lot, but they have nothing on Silas. That boy can pack it in.

Casey and Bo are on kitchen cleanup duty, so I'm waiting for him in his room. I brought my stuff for a facial tonight because I haven't had a chance to get one recently and it's definitely time.

Casey's bathroom isn't connected to his room, and he shares it with Bo and Silas, but surprisingly, it's pretty clean. Casey's probably the messiest out of the three, but he seems to keep it to his room. His closet specifically. I think his entire wardrobe is on the floor in there.

While I can't do my entire routine, I can accomplish what I need to do. And this isn't the first time Casey has seen me in a mask. I grab the little bag I brought over and set it on the bed. I'm pulling out my face wash and mask cream when he walks into the room.

"Whatcha got there, pretty girl?" He comes over to stand next to me.

"I haven't had a chance to go get a facial, and my skin needs a boost, so I brought my stuff over here. Figured I could put it on before we start a movie or something." I place my bag on his dresser behind me and walk back to the bed and sit down. "Do you think the guys are done using the bathroom for a while? I don't want to go in if they still need it."

"Nah, I think they're good. They're both watching TV in the family room, and Charlie and Beck went to their room to watch something and crash. Do you want me to grab a towel for you?" He walks to his closet and pulls a clean towel from the shelf.

"Thank you. I need to put my hair up real quick before I start." I get up and walk back to my bag. "Forgot to pull out my brush."

"Do you want me to braid your hair?" he asks.

Casey braids my hair often, which might seem weird to outsiders, but I love it. There have even been times I've fallen asleep while he was braiding. And he's pretty good at it too. Having a sister had something to do with it, I'm sure.

"Um, yes, please." I hand over the brush. "Where do you want me to sit?"

"I'll sit on the bed if you want to sit on the floor. Or you can sit on the bed and I can kneel behind you."

As soon as he says it, a visual of Casey on his knees for me runs through my thoughts.

Trey and I had sex a lot, but what he said to me that day has been playing in a loop in my mind, so now I feel like I've been thinking about sex more than I normally do. What if I do suck at sex, and that's why he was going behind my back? I would be mortified if I was doing something wrong. He was my first everything, so I just took his lead, but we never did anything like what he was doing with Zoey that day. There was no hair pulling or dirty talk. There was a little kissing, he might or might not go down on me, and then we'd have sex.

Maybe I am a little inexperienced in some regard. I'm not really sure if I've had an orgasm before. I bet Casey is good in bed. I've thought about it from time to time over the years. More out of curiosity than anything, but lately, it's been happening more and more and I'm trying to make sense of it.

"Noelle, where do you want me?" he asks again.

"Oh, sorry. I'll sit on the floor so you don't have to put any strain on your knees."

I squat down and plop down on the floor at the end of the

bed. I feel Casey sit down behind me. I can smell the detergent on his sweats and the clean smell of his soap and shampoo.

"You ready for tomorrow?" I ask him to break up the silence.

"Hell yeah. Speaking of the game, do you still have the jersey I got you last year that you only wore once? The one with my name on it specifically?" He pulls out the elastic from my hair and starts running the brush through it.

"Yeah. Why?"

"Well, I was thinking with you being my girlfriend and all, you should probably wear it to the game tomorrow."

I can feel that he's starting to separate the pieces to braid.

It's probably a good thing he can't see my face right now because every time he calls me his girlfriend, I can feel my face flush. I'm trying to hold in a smile, too, but I can't stop it.

"Yeah, you're right. I should definitely wear it. Make that statement, right?"

"It would be a good step toward making people believe it, and it wouldn't hurt to get them talking so it got back to Trey. You know some of those groupie girls will circle it around." He's halfway down my head.

"Okay, yeah, I'll wear it for sure. Although I would anyway. You got it for me late in the season, so I really only had a few chances to wear it. I gotta support my bestie." I laugh.

"You mean, your boyfriend. When we're in public, you'll have to start referring to me as your boyfriend. We should probably talk about our boundaries. Or rather your boundaries. I have none when it comes to you."

I can feel he's nearly done because he's at the base of my neck now.

"None, huh?" I laugh lightly.

"None. Ask me, and I'll probably do it." He wraps the elastic around the bottom of the braid, then puts his hands on my shoulders and squeezes gently.

"Careful, King. I might try to talk you into giving me a

massage too." I place my hand on the top of his hand on my right shoulder and tap it.

"I don't mind giving you a massage. You want it before or after the face-mask thing?"

He swings his leg over my head and stands. When he stands in front of me, he takes my hands in his and pulls me up from the floor.

Once I'm standing, he pulls me in closer to his chest.

Strong. Firm. Familiar.

His eyes haven't left mine. "So, how about those boundaries?"

"What boundaries?" My mind feels a little muddled by his intense gaze.

"Like, how, when, and where I can touch you."

"You're right; we should talk about it. I mean, I feel like we're pretty comfortable with each other as friends so I don't know that it will feel like a weird thing. At least not to me." I shrug, and that part I am sincere about. Hugging, holding hands … those are pretty natural things for us.

"We'll probably have to kiss in front of people at some point; otherwise, they might not buy it."

As he speaks, flutters run rampant in my stomach. Kissing Casey. The amount of times I've wondered … but I also don't want to embarrass myself if what Trey said is true and I don't know what I'm doing.

"How do you feel about kissing me?"

He's still holding my hands, and I'm close enough to count his eye lashes. His brown eyes are holding me captive, and I feel like I can't form words.

"Like, right now? Kissing you now?" My voice must sound like a chipmunk.

He laughs and steps back. I immediately want to be close to him again.

"We could kiss now if you feel like you're ready for that." He wiggles his eyebrows to try to lighten the sudden tension in the room.

"Well, I was gonna do my facial, but I could wait." *What the actual hell am I thinking?* "Ha! I mean, we can if you want to," I squeak.

His smile widens, and he winks at me. "Take a deep breath. We'll start with baby steps. I have an idea. Why don't we start with getting some pics together for Instagram to start building our story?"

"Oh, that's a good idea. Although I already have a lot of pictures of us together." I pull my phone from my back pocket and pull up the app. "See, it's mostly us. I deleted all the pictures I had with Trey."

"Has he tried to DM you there since you blocked his number on your phone?" He nods to my phone.

I shake my head. "No, but I blocked him there too."

"You should give me a facial. We'll do, like, a couples facial or something. Or is that stupid? I feel like Charlie and Beck do weird stuff like that all the time." He walks to his closet and pulls another towel off the shelf.

"That's a good idea." I nod.

"You'll have to put it on me though. I have no idea what I'm doing."

He turns toward the door, and I quickly swipe the cleanser and mask from the bed.

"Okay, let me do mine first, I guess, and then I'll do yours." I follow him into the bathroom.

As we cross the hallway, I can hear the TV in the other room and Bo and Silas talking about the game they're watching. It seems like they're occupied, so they won't be paying attention to us anyway, so I don't close the door when I enter.

"Sounds good to me. Do I just use this cleaner first?" He takes it from my hand.

"Yes, use this first. Oh, do you have any washcloths? I don't think I've ever seen any around, but it would be good to scrub your face a little to open up your pores and clean all the dirt off." I motion to my face and twirl my finger.

"Uh, I don't have any, but Charlie does. But, shit, I don't want to go in their room. I've more than learned my lesson. Let me text her instead." He winces and pulls his phone from his pocket. "While we wait ... do you want a water or anything?"

"Did Arbor leave any of those sparkling waters here?" I ask.

"I'll look. If we don't have any, you want something else? I think we have some Dr. Pepper." He moves around me and stands in the doorway, one brow lifted.

"Oh, yeah, for sure. I was just trying to avoid caffeine since it's getting late. But DP sounds good." I smile. "Thanks."

While he's gone, I take a good look at myself in the mirror. I wonder what he sees when he looks at me. I feel like I'm fairly ... common. I'm not short, but not tall either. But next to Casey and his six-feet-two size, I look much shorter. I have long brown hair. I have hazel eyes and long eyelashes. I never have to wear mascara because of it, which I love. And I'm not exactly the girl who dresses up to go out or go hang out with friends. I dress mostly like I do now. Comfortable. I have leggings and a cropped long-sleeved T-shirt that hangs off the shoulder a little. Not much fills out my sports bra, but that's okay with me.

Casey walks back in a few minutes later with two washcloths and two sparkling waters in hand. "There were exactly two left! And Charlie saved me from having to knock on their door since she wasn't answering my text."

I watch him in the mirror as he stands behind me, then reaches around to place the cans and the washcloths on the counter. He's got to be the handsomest guy I've ever seen. And, yes, I've known this all along. My best friend is *very* attractive. Yet, from the day we formed our bond, that moment when I realized the friendship was stronger than any other feelings that existed, that attraction became a moot point.

"Is your phone still in your pocket?" he asks, looking over my shoulder.

I nod.

"Take it out. I have an idea, but I have to know if you trust me first. Do you trust me?" He's not smiling, but there's a heated look in his eye.

"You know I trust you." I pull out my phone and lift it up for him to grab, but he doesn't.

Instead, he reaches behind his neck and pulls his shirt off. Defined arms and abs for days. He tosses it on the counter between the two sinks. He leans in closer, and I can feel the heat coming off his body.

"Lift your phone and take a pic of us in the mirror when I say. And at any time, if you're uncomfortable, tell me, and I'll stop."

"Okay," I breathe, my body tingling with an odd sense of anticipation.

He wraps one arm around my waist, his skin on mine. Then he brings his other arm across my chest, but above my breasts. When I look at his face in the mirror, he's watching me back. He's so close that I can feel his heated skin against my back and his light breath tickling my ear.

The longer we stare, the faster my heart beats. There's no way he doesn't notice.

With his eyes locked on mine, his hand on my chest starts to slide lower. "You good?"

I literally couldn't speak right now if I tried, so I just give a slight nod.

When my eyes start to move to watch his hand, he whispers in my ear, "Eyes on me, pretty girl."

My gaze snaps back to his, and when I feel his hand cup my breast, I take a deep breath in. It might sound lame, but this is probably the sexiest moment I've ever had.

He lifts his brow in question, and when I give him a soft smile, he says, "Now."

I tap the button on my phone once, twice.

He lifts his head from behind my ear, but his hands take their time drifting across my skin. I nearly grab his hand and put it back on my breast, but I don't. Because watching his hands move across my body feels just as good. He places a kiss on the back of my head and steps back, dropping his hands to his sides.

He clears his throat. "Should we put on the masks?"

Before he moves from behind me, I see him adjust himself in the mirror. Maybe he's just as affected as I am.

I look at my own face in the mirror, and I look like a puppet. My mouth is practically hanging open.

I close my eyes and shake my head to bring me back to task. "The masks. Right. Yes."

He doesn't laugh at my awkwardness. He turns his head from the mirror and looks at me, so I follow. When our eyes meet, he gives me a soft smile. When I return it, his smile widens, and he taps the counter.

"Okay then. Let's do this."

But I'm not sure if he's talking about the masks or us. Either way, I'm ready for it.

CASEY

WE HAVE A HOME GAME TODAY. It's the first time slot of the day, and we're on national TV. All of our games our televised, but ours is the game of the week. And with us being the reigning national champions, there's a certain amount of pressure that goes along with the expectation to have another great season.

Music is thumping through the speakers in the locker room, kicking up the adrenaline. We all have our own little rituals. Some guys bounce around the room, getting in each other's faces, and other guys sit with their headphones on.

My specific routine is done at home before the game. Since I've been playing football—or at least when I realized I might have some actual talent—I've kept notebooks that have every play I've run. We have so many that we memorize for each season and each game. So, I like to write out all the offensive drills in my notebook so I can see it in my head. Sometimes, I just sketch out the plays I'm running, but occasionally, I add other scenarios and where I need to be during those plays. I have three notebooks now here on campus with me. One for each season.

Beck's locker is next to mine, and as always, he's pretty quiet before games. He's got his headphones on and bobbing his head to the beat of whatever he's listening to. One of our athletic trainers, Sarah, is taping up his wrists.

"Can you wrap my ankles too?" he asks her.

"Yep, you got it." She looks up at me, brows raised. "How are you doing, Casey? You need anything from me?"

I hold out my hands and circle my wrists. "Yeah, but let's just do my ankles and my right wrist."

She nods, then starts wrapping Beck's ankles.

Neither of us has had any significant injuries over the years, but as offensive players who carry the ball, it's smart to protect our wrists and ankles. I even have them tape over my shoes so they don't get pulled off by defense trying to slow me down. It's happened. Shoe came right off, and my ass had to keep running. I was lucky I stayed on my feet at all.

"Okay, Beck, you're all set." Sarah stands. "Your turn, King."

I sit down on my bench in front of my locker and hold my leg out to her to start on my ankles first. "Can you go ahead and wrap around my shoes too?"

"Yep, no problem. You gonna get the ball today?" She looks up at me and smiles.

"That's the plan, Sar. Run that baby all the way down the field." I hold out my fist to Beck, who still has his headphones on, but he taps me anyway.

She finishes up my feet and moves to wrap my wrist. We make small talk while she works. She's been with us since our freshman year, so she's become part of the team in all the ways that count.

When she's finished, she stands and pats my shoulder. "Good luck today."

"Sarrrrahhhh!" someone across the locker room calls for her.

I smile and nod. "Thanks. Maybe we'll see you at the neon party at Schuster and Smith's."

"Ha! Maybe, but not likely." She smiles and grabs her kit.

We're about twenty minutes to game time when Coach comes into the locker room.

"Okay, guys, let's bring it in." He holds up his hand and waves us toward him. "Today, we need to stay focused. We need to communicate and execute. Kansas runs a high-powered offense, but we're better. Let's get out there and show them what it takes to be a champion! Stallions on three."

Our offensive coordinator is standing next to him and leads the count. "One, two, three, Stallions!"

"Stallions!" we collectively chant.

I walk back to my locker, Beck next to me. "You ready to go, man?" I ask him.

He nods. "I'm ready. You ready, King?"

"I'm ready!" I shout. "Let's fucking go!"

We all walk out and make our way through the tunnel, where we listen to the roar of the crowd inside the stadium as we wait for the team to be called to the field. The band is playing, and the mascots are lined up and waiting.

It's time to go.

When we run out, we go to the sidelines and drop our gear. I look into the stands to find my family, but I'm also looking for Noelle. She's supposed to be sitting with my sister and her friends today. And I hope she's wearing my jersey.

I spot my parents and wave, then move my gaze down their row to where my sister should be. They're in the third row back, but I spot my sister and Noelle in the front row, waving to me. Beck passes by and heads straight to my sister. She leans over and kisses him.

When I get to them, Noelle has a soft smile on her face, cheeks slightly pink, wearing ... my jersey.

"Hey," I say, lifting my arm up to reach her hand.

She leans over and takes my hand in hers, smiling. "Hello, Casey King."

I laugh. "Hello, Noelle James. Nice jersey."

"Thank you. Red looks good on me," she teases. "You gonna get a touchdown today?"

"You know it. I just need Callaway to give me the ball."

"Definitely, but seriously, you feel okay?" she asks.

"I feel fired up. I'm ready to go." I smile at her.

"Okay, well … good luck." She's looking at me, brows raised.

"Hey, come here. Lean over as far as you can." I get as close to the wall as I can and lean up to meet her.

When her face is in front of mine, I place my hand on her cheek. "Thank you for coming today."

She smiles and nods. "I mean, of course. That's what girl-friends do, right?"

"Yeah, I guess they do. But no one looks as good in my number as my girlfriend does." I turn my head to graze her cheek with my lips. "I'll see you later, pretty girl."

As I pull back, I bring her hand up and kiss it. Then I turn and get ready to win.

We're up by one touchdown, and there is four minutes, thirty-two seconds left on the clock. We have the field, and Beck just ran for a first down. In the huddle, Bo makes the next call.

"Okay, boys, let's wrap this up. I'm getting sick of smelling Thorton every time he comes at me. He fucking stinks." I'm standing next to him, and he puts a hand on my shoulder. "Here we go. Trip right, eighty-two. All go. Break."

We all clap.

This call brings three receivers to the right of the field, running deep, with me as the intended target. We line up and wait for Bo's call. My hands are loose at my sides. I look to my left, then my right, watching the defense to see if they can read our play.

"Red fourteen. Red fourteen. Hut!"

The ball snaps, my feet dig in, and then I take off. There are three of us running down the right side of the field, trying to keep the defense off of us. I turn my body to see where Bo is, just as he launches the ball in my direction. There's a cornerback on my heels so I hold out my arm to try to keep him off of me. The ball is within my reach, but with this guy on my tail, I only have one hand free. Reaching up, I grab the ball from the air and grip it as tight as I can, tucking it tightly into my side. And then I run.

I've already passed the first down marker, so I'm going all the way into the end zone. In my peripheral vision, I see two of their players coming at me from the side, so I pivot, dig my foot in the grass, and run it in.

In the end zone, I hold the ball out with one hand and nod. I'm not usually one to showboat much, but this one feels good. My teammates jump on me and smack my helmet.

I toss the ball to the ref, then run back to the sideline.

Coach grabs my arm and leans in. "That's what I want to see, King! That's what I want to see in every game. Quick feet, smart thinking. Good job, kid!"

"Thanks, Coach." I nod and walk off.

When I get to the bench, I look up to the stands and see Noelle on her feet, next to my sister, clapping. I point to her and wink, which makes her smile.

She might be my fake girlfriend, but that girl in the stands cheering me on … looks like mine.

CHAPTER
TEN

THE THIRD-GRADE CLASS I get to teach this year at Arrow Cross Elementary is so much fun already. There's a great teacher in the classroom with me, but she's allowing me to get as much hands-on experience as I can.

I've been home for a few hours, knee deep in lesson plans. Once I submit them to the teacher I'm working with and she approves them, I'll add them to my portfolio that will count toward my final grade at the end of the semester.

It doesn't usually take me this long to complete the lesson plans, but I feel very distracted with thoughts of Casey. I think back to our friendship in high school specifically. I remember the gift he gave me for my seventeenth birthday. With my birthday falling around Christmas, I don't always get separate gifts. This one I did though. He gave me a book of poems about friendship, called *When I Think About You, My Friend*. I loved it because I could tell he'd put some thought into it.

But what really made it special was the handwritten card he'd placed in the book sleeve.

After I opened the box with the book inside, he placed his

hand on top of mine and asked me to look through it when I was alone. I remember taking it upstairs after he left, and I found the card. In it, he told me how much my friendship meant to him and how he hoped we would always be in each other's lives. For a teenage boy, it was pretty deep, now that I think back on it. And then at the bottom, above his signature, he told me he loved me. At the time, I didn't think much of it because we would say *I love you* to each other occasionally, joking and with an eye roll, as friends do.

My phone buzzes with a text, shaking me from my thoughts, but I can't find it. Papers cover the small kitchen table we have in our apartment, so my phone is likely hiding somewhere under this pile. When I locate it under my spiral planner, I see Casey has texted a few times. These last two are telling me he's on his way over to my apartment.

I jump up from my chair and run into the bathroom. I'm not sure when I started to care about what I looked like in front of Casey, but here we are. Could be because of all the pictures we've been taking together. Most of which he's been taking and posting first. He says we need to make it look as real as we can. Hard launch. Instagram official.

The funny thing is, none of his close friends or even his sister seems to think our fake relationship is odd. It's almost like it's always been this way, which I guess we have been. Even when I was with Trey.

I'm in my room, pulling on a different shirt and swiping some deodorant on quickly when I hear a knock at the door. I glance in the mirror on my way out and see my hair looking like a complete disaster. Ponytail it is.

When I open the door, Casey is peering down at me from under the lid of his baseball hat. His hand is bracing the doorframe, accentuating his long torso and broad chest. Casey looks good in anything he wears, and it's something that I've been noticing more and more. Right now, he's wearing gym shorts and a long-sleeved Walker football shirt. Jeans and a button-down, prom suit, football uniform—all hot looks. But when he's casual like this, I feel like I have to catch myself from staring nonstop.

I've always felt good, just being around him, but now that he's pretending to be mine, I can't help but wonder what it would be like for us to really be together.

"Hey." He pushes off the doorframe. "Thought I'd come rescue you from lesson plans for a Classic '50s break. I'm craving a cherry limeade," he says as he walks into my apartment.

A slushy does sound good, and Classic '50s has the best. It's an old-school drive-in that is a Walker staple. They not only have the best slushies, but the food is superior fast food, and the servers deliver your order on roller skates. One of my favorites, until Trey, was Frito chili pie. It's so freaking good, but he basically called me fat for eating it, talking about how bad it was for me, so I haven't had it since our freshman year.

"Yum, that does sound good. Let me go grab my shoes." I go back to my room and put on my sneakers without laces so I can slide them on easily.

When I come out, Casey is looking over my lesson plans. He has a smile on his face, and he's pointing to one of the notebooks. "Noelle ... did you doodle my name on your homework?"

I laugh because he said *doodle*. "Nooo. I mean, yes, but not in the way you think. I wrote it there because I was thinking about you." I duck my head and reach across the table so he can't see the blush on my face, and I grab my keys from my bag.

"You were thinking about me?" I can hear the smile in his voice. It's genuine and not teasing. Like he's happy I was thinking about him.

"Yes, I was wishing you would come rescue me from lesson plans for a slushy, and, poof, here you are! Manifestation works, Casey. I've told you this for years." I grab his hand and pull him toward the door.

"So, you manifested me taking you out on an official date to

The Font? Because we're gonna do that this week too. The full treatment, and you know there are eyes all over the place there. Someone is sure to see us."

I stop at the door to look at his face to see if he's serious or teasing me. He's smiling, but he's not kidding.

"Oh, I mean, yeah, that would be perfect. And you know I love The Font."

"It's a date then." He winks, then passes by me in the doorway so I can lock the door.

Fifteen minutes later, we pull up into an empty spot at the drive-in.

Casey presses the button to place the order, and while we wait, he asks, "Your usual?"

"Yep, I want blue coconut, but I think I'll switch things up a little and do gummy worms instead of bears." I drop my mouth open in mock surprise, making him laugh.

"Living on the edge tonight. I like it!" the girl on the speaker interrupts, and he places our drink order.

As we wait for our order, he tells me about his practice today. I think he likes to tell me about the plays they run, more for his own benefit of memorizing them because I've never understood a single word.

I just nod and give the occasional, "Oh wow."

While he talks tonight though, I can't help but watch his mouth. His lips are perfect—full, lush, kissable. And I wonder what they would feel like on mine. I wonder what he would do if I leaned over and tangled my lips with his right now. I wonder if he would kiss me back. I wonder … if he would like it.

Before my brain catches up to my thoughts, I blurt out, "I think we should kiss."

A slow smile spreads on his face, but before he can say anything, the girl rolls up with our slushies.

"A cherry limeade and a blue coconut with worms. Let me know if you need anything else." She rolls away as fast as she arrived.

Casey hands me my cup, and I take a sip, but I'm still watching his face. I mean, I put it out there, and I can't take it back, so I need to read his expression.

"Aren't you just full of surprises tonight, pretty girl? First worms, now a kiss, huh?" He takes my drink from my hand and puts both of our cups in the drink holders.

"I mean, we don't have to. I just figured it might be easier to have our first in private. But, no, we shouldn't—"

"Oh, no. We're going to. But I am curious. Do you want to kiss me so it looks real to other people, or do you want to kiss me because you want to taste me as much as I want to taste you?"

The rush of heat that shoots through my body is nothing like I've ever experienced before. And now, of course, I can't find my words, so I nod.

"You need to speak, Noelle."

I swallow, and my words come out hoarse. "The second one."

"Well then … let's do this."

One of his hands slides around my neck, and he pulls me toward him. I look between his lips and eyes as we get closer. Instead of placing his lips on mine, he kisses my forehead, then trails kisses down the side of my face, on my neck, then along my jaw until he reaches my mouth.

He pulls back slightly to look me in the eyes. "I've been waiting a really long time for this."

Before I can ask him what he means, he places the most perfect, softest kiss on my lips. He pulls back and searches my eyes. When he leans back in, he angles his head and traces his tongue along the seam of my lips.

My lips part instinctively for him, and our tongues meet for the first time. It starts off slow and gentle, our tongues dancing around each other. With his tongue caressing my own, I feel a wave of pleasure roll down my body and settle in my core. His lips are firm, his tongue like satin, and there's something so passionate about the way his hand pulls me in and his breath comes out like a moan. I am so lost in this kiss that I forget my name. Then a car horn beeps, startling us both.

We pull apart, but our faces are still aligned.

"I don't know about you, but I wouldn't mind doing more of that." He kisses the tip of my nose, one cheek, and then the other.

"Oh, we'll definitely do more of that. Since you're my boyfriend and all." *Who is this breathy girl speaking? It's like I've lost all sense because of Casey King's lips.*

He releases my head and pulls away, then winks. "Damn straight I am." And it doesn't sound fake at all.

CASEY

A FEW DAYS LATER, I pick up Noelle to take her on our first official date. She might think this is for show, but for me, it's not. I want to show her what it would be like to date me for real. Show her how she deserves to be treated.

She's waiting outside her apartment, and she waves when she sees me and starts to walk toward the car. I get out anyway —because I respect women.

When she reaches me, I pull her in for a hug and kiss her forehead. "Hey, you. Were you excited to see me? Waiting outside and everything."

She laughs. "Well, you texted me when you left your place, so I timed it and thought I'd just be ready when you got here. Plus, Chelsea is studying, and I don't want to interrupt her."

"I like the idea that you were excited to see me better."

We walk to the passenger side of my truck, and I open the door and hold out my hand for her as she climbs up.

"Always a gentleman." She smiles her genuine, gorgeous smile.

"That's right. My parents taught me well."

And that's true. My dad was a great role model, but my mom also expected me to open her doors when my dad wasn't around. So, it's just something that was standard in my family. Respect and treat women kindly.

"They did good."

I nod and shut her door, then walk around to the driver's side. "What are you hungry for? We haven't been to The Font in a while. I can't decide what to get yet."

"Hmm … I haven't decided yet either. So many choices. I'll probably go with, like, a Reuben or enchiladas. I'll have to see what my tummy tells me once we get there."

"Enchiladas sound good. So does the queso burger, but I'll probably end up with the low-carb dinner."

She shoots me a thumbs-down. "That's boring though, Case. You can't go to The Font and not get something on the greasy side. It's just not right."

"As soon as the season is over, I'll get all the greasy goodness. I have to get a run in tomorrow though, and I always feel like crap if I don't eat well the night before."

"Okay, well, I'll enjoy it for both of us." She smiles and nods.

A few minutes later, we pull into a parking spot. I get out, round the car, and open her door. When her feet hit the ground, I don't let go of her hand. She looks at our joined hands and smiles.

We get seated at a smaller table, which works for me because I want to be close to her. I spot a few people I recognize, so, yeah, this is perfect.

I take her hand in mine and rest them on the table. "So, tell me about your day."

"Casey, you just saw me after my last class."

"I know, but what did you do after you got home?" I rub my thumb across the top of her hand.

"Well, I took a power nap for, like, twenty minutes. Then I reviewed my assignments for tomorrow. Checked my lesson plans, then submitted them to my mentor. Talked to Chelsea for a few minutes, then waited for you to pick me up." She clears her throat. "I did get a text from Trey."

"And?" I wave my hand for her to tell me more.

"It was a picture of you and me kissing at Classic '50s. It looked like someone from a few cars over took the pic." She shakes her head and pulls her hand back.

"Good. Did he say anything else? Did you answer him?" I raise my brows questioningly.

"He just asked if it was real. I didn't answer and blocked him again." She shrugs. "He keeps texting from unknown numbers."

"Funny to me that his buddies care enough to take a pic of us and send it to Trey." I clap my hands together and chuckle.

The waitress comes over and sets menus on the table, interrupting our conversation. "Can I get y'all something to drink while you look at the menu?"

"Oh, hey, Greer. I didn't know you worked here now." Noelle's smile drops.

"Noelle? Oh my God, I didn't even recognize you. How are you?" She gives Noelle a fake smile.

"Um, I'm doing good. Busy with school and stuff."

"Oh, hey, I'm sorry to hear about you and Trey. That was really shitty of Zoey to do that to you." Greer gives Noelle a pout.

I can't help but interrupt. "Noelle got an upgrade. Trust me, she's not missing Trey." I take Noelle's hand in mine again.

She looks at me, then at Noelle. "Well then, yay, you! And a star football player, no less. Well done, Noelle. You get all the good ones."

"I wouldn't exactly call Trey a good one though, would you?" I press.

She laughs, but it's forced. "No, you're right. I just meant good-looking guys."

"Right. How about those drinks, Gwen?" I smile at her.

"It's Greer," she sneers.

I wave my free hand. "Whatever. My girl here will have a Dr. Pepper, and I'll have a water with lemon."

"I'll be right back with those drinks." She spins on her heel and walks away.

When I look at Noelle, she's smiling. "What?" I ask her.

"Nothing. I just think you're funny." She giggles.

"Oh, yeah? Why am I funny?" I cup her hand with both of mine.

She smiles but tucks her head. "A lot of the guys who play baseball are obsessed with her. And from what I hear, she's made her rounds with other athletes. But you totally blew her off. Surely, you think she's pretty."

"Noelle, I don't see anyone but you." I move one hand to her chin and tilt it, then lean across the table and kiss her. "But even if I did see her, I wouldn't find her attractive because of her lack of sincerity when she was speaking to you. You know I can't stand fake people, and she's, like, the leader."

"Leader of the fake people," she repeats and laughs.

I look over Noelle's shoulder to see Greer on her phone. "She's texting right now. I hope she's telling everyone you're here with me." I look back at Noelle. "Should we give them something to talk about?"

"What do you mean?" She tilts her head in question.

I pull her chair right next to mine and put my arm around the back. Then I cup her cheek and turn her face toward mine. "I mean, I'm gonna kiss you. And I want everyone in here to see it."

"Okay," she whispers against my lips.

Then I kiss her. And I don't stop kissing her the entire time we're there. Because for me, nothing about this is fake, and I'm going to take advantage of every chance she gives me to show her how good we can be together.

CHAPTER
TWELVE

"DATING" one of Walker's star football players definitely has its perks. Since the last game, when Casey kissed my cheek, which made it onto social media, the baristas at the campus coffee shop have been overly friendly. And if Casey is with me, people we don't know nod and say hello when they pass. It's a little weird. Even though Trey was an athlete, the football players here are treated like royalty.

Case in point, I walk out of my last class of the day and see Casey standing at the end of the walkway, talking to a very pretty blonde. I mean, she's looking at him like she'd get on her knees right here in the middle of campus. And I have to say … I don't like it. Because the more we act like a couple, the more my feelings are changing into something more than friendship.

Jealousy doesn't look good on me, so I try to suck in these feelings because, really, I have no real claim on Casey.

As I walk toward them, he turns and sees me. The friendly smile he was giving her is replaced by the smile I love and know is genuine. I wonder what he would do if I leaned in to kiss him in front of this girl.

The thought of kissing him has nearly consumed all my thoughts since the other night. I want to kiss him again desperately, but he hasn't made a move since our date night. I mean, why would he? It's not like we're really dating.

"Hey," he says, walking up to me.

I look over to the girl he just walked away from and see she's glaring at me with a fake smile. Maybe I shouldn't be so happy he didn't give her a second glance, but I am. So, when he reaches me, I lift up on my toes and wrap my arms around him.

"Hi," I say as I pull back. "Was she part of your fan club?"

He laughs and wraps his arm around my shoulders as we start walking. "I mean, she might be the president. Who knows?"

"Right, right." I know he's joking, but still, I don't like it. "So, I was thinking, do you want to come over tonight? I'll make dinner, and we can watch a movie or something."

"Yeah, that sounds good. Do you want me to come straight from practice?" He drops his arm from my shoulders, but grabs my hand.

"That works. Anything in particular that you want to eat?" I look up at his face.

He smirks and bites his bottom lip. "Uhhh, yeah. But I'm not sure we're at that stage in our relationship yet."

"What do you—" The heat that rushes to my face must be noticeable as I finally *get* his meaning.

Oh my.

There's no way I can hide this reaction I'm having to the visual that just popped into my head, but also, this could be my chance to bring up something I've been thinking about.

I clear my throat to remove the frog in my voice. When we're outside and away from prying ears, I broach the topic. "Speaking of what I think you're referring to, I was wondering if maybe you could help me with something." The butterflies in my stomach right now are insane.

He stops walking and turns to me. "What do you think I'm talking about, Noelle?"

There's a soft smile on his face, so I know he's not mocking me.

"Well, I assume you mean sexy things, right?" I squeeze his hand.

His free hand comes to the side of my face, and he tilts his head, eyes roaming my face. "What do you need, pretty girl?"

"Something Trey said the last time I saw him hasn't left my mind." I shake my head and look down, hiding my embarrassment for what I'm about to say. "I know it's stupid, and I really shouldn't care, but he blamed me for cheating. He said if I knew what I was doing in the bedroom, he wouldn't have had to hook up with Zoey."

When Casey's hand falls from my face and he doesn't say anything, I look up. His jaw is clenched, and his fists tighten like he can punch through a wall, and Casey isn't that type of guy.

"He said that to you? Why didn't you tell me that before?"

"I mean, because I don't really want to admit to anyone that I'm not good in bed."

I try to pull my hand from his, but he doesn't let me.

"Uh-uh. No. Anything that douchebag said to you was a fucking lie—you have to know that by now, right?" He takes my other hand in his.

I sigh. "Honestly, Casey, I'm not so sure about this though. I was confident, but the last few weeks I've been replaying his words in my head. You know he's the only guy I've ever been with. Maybe I don't know what I'm doing, you know?" I shrug.

Casey tilts his head back and closes his eyes. "I can't even think about you with him. Can we not go into detail about the things you did together?"

I'm not really sure what to say to that because I'm confused about whether he doesn't want to think about me like that, or maybe, just maybe, he might not like the thought of me with someone else either.

"Okay, I won't give details then …" I swallow.

"What did you want help with, exactly?"

"I'm not entirely sure. Maybe explain to me what you like in bed. I can tell you what I think is the right way to do it. Maybe we can break out a banana, and you show me what you like. I want to know what turns you on."

"What turns *me* on."

"Yeah, well, I mean … men. In general. Not you, per se."

He runs a hand over his jaw and studies my expression, which I'm sure is a mix of mortification and desperation with a heavy dose of expectation. "I feel like you're not saying something that you really want to say."

"What if you taught me how to, you know, do things?" I add.

His head snaps back up, and his eyes are wide. "Just to be very fucking clear here, you are asking me to give you, like, sex lessons?"

I laugh nervously because hearing it said like that … yeah, awkward. "I mean, yeah, I guess."

"You want it with a banana and, what, like, a diagram?"

"Perhaps some descriptive conversation? I'm sure the best way for me to learn is for you to actually get naked with me and tell me if I'm lame in bed, but I don't ever want to compromise our friendship, and I know I'm asking a lot already by having you pretend to be my boyfriend, but if there's anyone I would feel comfortable doing this with, it's you." I pull in a deep breath, suddenly feeling like I can't get enough air.

"I like your idea."

"What idea?"

"Getting naked with you."

"You'd do that with me?" I ask incredulously. "Like, seriously have sex with me?"

"Yes." His answer is so straightforward that I have to blink to see if he means it.

"I don't need a pity fuck."

He takes a step closer. His expression turns serious as he

looks down at me with that intense gaze. "Trust me when I say, you're the one who is doing me the favor here."

I bite down on my lower lip and feel the tingles roll through my body at the realization that I just may be getting naked with Casey, which means I get to feel him. *All of him.*

His hands release mine, and he frames my face, sliding his hands into my hair. "Noelle James, it would be an honor to fuck you."

For a minute, I think he's going to lean in and get started right here in the quad. His eyes … yeah, I mean, I'm clearly not an expert, but they kind of have that look like that day in the bathroom when he was holding my breast.

"Okay, great. I mean, thank you. This is good." I stumble over my words. "So, like, should we start tonight? We'll be there alone. Chelsea has to tutor tonight."

He drops his hands from my face and laughs. "Anxious to get started, yeah?"

"Well, I mean, I feel like now is the time to seize the moment and whatnot, right?" I smile because this whole thing is so out of the ordinary for me that I can't help my own ridiculousness.

"Are you sure about this? Don't get me wrong; I'm on board, but I want you to be sure—because once we do this, I won't want to stop." His smile falls, and his face turns serious.

When I look at him now, he seems less like my best friend and more like someone I can't wait to see naked. So, yes, I'm absolutely sure. "One hundred percent sure."

CASEY

PRACTICE COULDN'T END FAST ENOUGH. I kept playing our conversation over and over in my mind, trying to figure out if I'd misheard her. But nope, she'd said it.

And I still can't believe Trey said that to her. I mean, I can, but what a fucking asshole. It's likely he just doesn't know what he's doing, so he blamed her. I bet he has a little dick too.

I took the fastest shower I ever had, and I know Beck, at the very least, knows something is up, but he's not as nosy as some of the other guys. He'll let me tell him when I'm ready.

"I'll see y'all later." I finish dressing and grab my bag, heading for the locker room door.

"Yo, where are you going?" Bo yells.

"I'm going over to Noelle's. Is that okay with you, Dad?" I laugh.

He tilts his head, then smirks. "Proceed. But be home by curfew, kid."

I salute him and keep walking. I make it to my truck, toss my bag into the passenger side, and pull out my phone. I shoot Noelle a text to let her know I'm on my way.

> Casey: On my way. Do you need me to bring anything?

> Noelle: Condoms?

I bark out a laugh. She can't be serious. Not that I don't want to because I absolutely do, but she's going from zero to a hundred.

> Casey: I'm not sure if you're serious or not, but I meant food.

> Noelle: *laughing emoji* I just wanted to see what you would say.

> Casey: I mean, I can bring some, but let's take this one step at a time, yeah?

> Noelle: See you soon.

I make my way to her place within ten minutes. As soon as I put the truck in park, I'm out the door. I'm not exactly running, but I'm not wasting time.

Honestly, I have no expectations for anything to happen. I think what has me the most anxious is that she actually wants this. For years, I've wanted her. And it could happen. Like, for real and not just in my fantasy.

Before I get to knock on the door, she's pulling it open.

"Hi!" she squeaks, and it's so fucking cute.

"Hi!" I bend down to hug her and kiss her cheek. I'm going to let her set the pace.

She takes my hand and pulls me into the apartment, releases my hand, then shuts the door and locks it. "Dinner is ready, and I figured you would be hungry after practice. I was going to cook, but then I kind of lost track of time, so I ordered food in."

I can't help but laugh. "It's okay. I'm good with whatever you got."

"Okay, I got you chicken, brown rice, and veggies. I wasn't sure what you would want or could eat, so I went with what I've seen you eat before." She's talking with her hands. She's nervous.

I take her hands in mine. "That sounds great. Thank you."

She looks down at our hands.

"Hey." I release one hand and tilt her chin up with my finger. "It's just me."

Taking hold of my wrist, she looks me in the eye. "I know. I don't mean to make things weird. Honestly, I'm"—she takes a deep breath and releases it—"excited."

Am I shocked? A little bit, yeah. I really never knew she even saw me that way. I thought I had been friend-zoned forever.

"Well, that's good to know. I am too."

"You are? Even though it's me, Noelle, who you've been friends with forever?" She smiles bashfully.

"I'm excited because it's *you*. I'm excited because you trust *me*. You want … *me*." I lean in closer to her and kiss her forehead.

"Case, I'm not a virgin. I know you don't want details of my past with Trey, but you don't have to have kid gloves with me."

"So, you're looking for the, what did you say … *wild, crazy* … what else was it?"

"*Raunchy*. That was because Trey is the only guy I've been with. And he didn't always like to do things. Foreplay things. He was a *wham, bam, thank you, ma'am* kinda guy, and I might have learned some bad habits. I'm sure most girls would go on a sexcapade after a big breakup and hook up around campus—"

"You are *not* hooking up with anyone on campus, let alone sleeping around."

She rolls those pretty hazel eyes. "Obviously. That's why I have you. So … no kid gloves. Manhandle me. Show me all the tricks, and if there's anything you've always wanted to try but haven't gotten to, I'm here to help you too."

I lift a brow and give her a smirk. "*Anything* I want to try?" I tease.

Her teeth gnaw on her bottom lip as she retracts. "Well … not *anything*. I'll keep an open mind though."

I laugh and kiss her again on the head because she's way too fucking cute to be this sexy. "If that's what you want. But understand that you will set the pace here. I don't want to do anything you aren't ready to share with me."

"And this is just one of the reasons why I want to do this with you. I can't lie and say it wasn't a little embarrassing to ask you to do this, but also … it kind of makes sense." She shrugs like it's not a big deal, but we both know it is.

"Let's eat. You need food in that stomach before you get all anxious and decide you won't eat a thing."

I take her over to the counter where she has the food set up. There are two stools, so I pull one out from under the counter for her to sit, then bring mine out.

She ordered a salad with grilled chicken and no dressing. It seems like her eating habits have gotten a little better since she broke up with Trey, but she still doesn't eat enough in my opinion.

As much as I want to drag her back into her room and get started, I also want her to relax. So, we talk about school, football, her new class she's student teaching in. I love hearing her talk about anything really, but when she talks about teaching, she lights up.

After we clean up our dishes, we move over to the couch. I lie down first, and then she lies against me so I can spoon her, her back to my front. She shimmies up against me like she's never done before—her tight little ass pressing against my dick in a way that makes my eyes roll to the back of my head.

When she lets out a shiver, I assume she's cold. I grab a blanket off the back of the couch and rest it over her. Me? I'm hot as fuck.

It's not unusual for us to cuddle up, but now I know there might be more that happens under the blanket. Managing my hard-on has always been a chore, but I'm busting out everything I can to keep my mind off her body against me.

She turns her head to look at me. "What do you want to watch?"

"I'm good with whatever. Are there any new movies out right now?" I prop my head on my hand and look at her.

"I feel like we've seen everything new, so maybe we pick something we've seen a hundred times." She laughs. "Oh, I know! We could watch the new season of *The Amazing Race*! I still think we could totally win that show."

"Yeah, let's put that on. And I agree. We would win for sure. I don't think Coach would appreciate me signing on for that though. Some of those tasks are hard-core." I laugh. "And you know how I feel about heights. You would have to be the one doing all those. I'll take care of the running parts. Hop on my back, and we'd be first every week."

"I would take anything with heights. They don't bother me at all."

She clicks on the show, and we start to watch and analyze every couple they introduce.

While it's typical of how we spend time together, the feel of her against me, along with the smell of her citrus shampoo, is driving me crazy. As much as I've tried to fight my hard-on, it has a mind of its own. There's no doubt she can feel it.

On the screen, a couple is running across a rickety wooden drawbridge. The music is that fast-paced kind that is supposed to make you nervous, thinking they won't make it safely to the other side. Instead of watching the show, I'm entranced by the woman lying in front of me and the way her breaths are a little too shallow for someone who should be lying here, relaxing.

Her hair is in a ponytail, leaving her neck exposed. I lift my finger and trace the exposed skin and run the pad of my finger from the lobe of her ear down to the nape of her neck and back.

She shivers again, and this time, I'm certain she's not cold.

"Casey ..." She brings her hand out of the blanket and grabs my hand that's caressing her neck. "I want you to kiss me like you did that night in the bathroom."

With our hands entwined, she moves them under the blanket. My arm is resting on her waist, and our hands are in front of her body, close to her chest.

I lean down slightly and kiss her neck behind her ear, just like I did that night in the bathroom. Soft, closed-mouthed kisses line her neck, and goose bumps follow.

Her breath hisses, and her hips buck.

"Keep kissing me there." Her voice is quiet, but I can feel the rise and fall of her chest. She's definitely getting as turned on as I am, and we haven't even really done anything.

Needing a taste, I lick her flesh and follow where I just kissed her. I suck lightly at some spots and feel her body react beneath me.

My other arm has been under the pillow, but I pull it out, which causes her to turn toward me slightly. The blanket falls to her waist with the movement, and I can see our hands resting together below her heart. I loosen my fingers from hers and brush my thumb back and forth across the underside of her breast.

She looks up at me, and without a word, I lean down and kiss my best friend for the second time. The minute our lips touch, it's like a match is lit.

Noelle releases my hand and brings both of her hands to my face, holding me in place. Not that I would be going anywhere. When I feel her tongue trace the seam of my lips, I nearly lose it.

Our tongues tangle together while my hand starts to roam. I want to touch her everywhere. In this position though, I can only use one hand, but I thread my other that's under her head through her loose ponytail.

When I slide my hand under her shirt, she doesn't stop me, so I continue and move to her breast. I pull the top of her sports bra down to expose her nipples and circle one with my finger. Breaking our kiss, I pull back, lift up her shirt, and look at her.

"I can't wait to taste these." I take her nipple between my thumb and forefinger and pinch, which causes her to gasp. "You like this?" I ask while I continue teasing her nipple.

She nods and bites down on her bottom lip.

I move my hand to her other breast and look down so I can see her peaked nipples. Her breasts are perfect, just the right size, fitting into my palm perfectly.

She pulls me back to her, and we get lost in our kiss again. I continue to knead, stroke, and pinch her breasts. Her hips are starting to circle, and I can't help but wonder if she's close to orgasming.

"Casey, please." She breaks the kiss, panting.

"What do you need, pretty girl?"

I place kisses along her jaw and move down to her chest, looking up to see her watching me. I tentatively lick one nipple, and when she doesn't stop me, I suck it completely into my mouth, making her moan.

"I need you to keep sucking on my nipples and touching them the way you do. I never knew I liked nipple play so much. It's intense," she gasps. "I ... I love it."

I reward her with a soft bite.

"That feels so good, Casey." Her hands are in my hair now, slightly pulling it. "Keep going."

I release her breast and drag my finger lightly over her stomach to the waistband of her shorts. I can see goose bumps appear on her skin, and she lifts her hips just enough to encourage me to keep going.

I slide my hand into her underwear. Memorizing the feel of her skin. I reach her center, and she opens her legs wide enough for me to fit my hand between her legs.

I rub her clit in circles with two fingers while I continue to suck on her nipples. Her breathing is heavier now, and I can feel her getting wetter. I slide my fingers down and into her, then back up to her clit. With a pop, I release her nipple and look at her face. She's watching me, those hazel eyes looking back at me hungrily.

She releases my head and runs her hands over my shoulders. One hand stays there while she moves the other down my arm and holds my forearm. Not to stop me though. She's bracing herself for anything that's about to happen.

"Touch yourself, Noelle. I'm gonna make you come with my hand on your pussy, but I want you to know your body. What feels good. You don't have to hide from me. Let me see you come undone." I lean down and kiss her lips.

She tries to deepen the kiss, but I pull back.

"Casey," she pleads.

"Trust me. Just feel your body while I make you come. Grab on to those perfect breasts of yours and play with the pink buds. You're so sensitive to my touch. I want to see you touch yourself."

My hand starts to move faster when she does take her breasts in her hands and kneads them. When she circles her nipples with her fingertips, I nearly come in my sweats.

"Just like that."

Her hips move in rhythm with my hand, and I can tell she's close. Her eyes are closed, her lips are parted, and her head is strained back, as if she wants to run from the ambush of sensations hitting her, yet from how her hips are pushing into my hand, I know she is chasing it just as hard.

My hand moves faster, the pressure firmer, and with a tease of my finger inside her pussy, I feel her body start to unravel.

I lean down and kiss her as her orgasm ripples through her body, and I push two fingers deep into her pussy, pumping while she rides it out.

"Holy shit, Case."

She pants as she comes all over my hand, her walls pulsating on my fingers as she grips them tight from the inside out. My dick is like steel at the thought of what it would be like to have myself buried deep inside her.

She's glowing, and that gorgeous smile of hers spreads across her face in a satisfied haze. "Now I know I've never had an orgasm before. I can feel it all the way to my toes. And we didn't even have sex." Her eyes are wide and mouth slightly open.

I pull my fingers from her center and circle her clit one more time. For good measure. Her body jolts as she groans for more, sensitive to the touch.

"I don't want to sound like I'm totally lost, but I've never had that experience before." She pushes up onto her elbows. "When can we do it again?"

"I'm all yours, whenever you want me." I kiss her again because I can. I don't think I'll ever get enough of her.

CHAPTER
FOURTEEN

THE TEAM HAS AN AWAY game this week, and Charlie invited me to come over to the house to watch the game with her, Arbor, and Lily. I'm bringing Chelsea with me too. She's not much of a sports fan, but she didn't have to work today for the first time in forever, so she agreed to come.

We're cutting it close time-wise and pull up about fifteen minutes before the game starts. I knock on the door, but open it without waiting for a response.

"Hey, y'all," I call out.

A collective, "Hey!" rings out.

Arbor and Lily are on the couch, beers in hand and popcorn on the table. I don't see Charlie. When I walk around the corner, I see her in the kitchen, putting some brownies in the oven. This girl loves baking. I swear there are either cookies or brownies sitting around here on a daily basis.

"Hey, you," she says as she closes the oven.

"Hi!" I walk over and give her a hug. "Thanks for inviting me over today."

"Girl, of course. I'm glad you came." She looks around me and smiles. "Hi, Chelsea."

"Hey, Charlie. Thanks for having me over too." Chelsea waves and smiles.

"It's game day, baby! All are welcome here at Casa King, as my brother would say."

She takes a bottle of soda out of the fridge and looks at us and offers us a drink.

"We have plenty of snacks, so help yourself. I ordered a few pizzas for us too. I don't get to eat a ton of junk food with the guys, so I like to live it up when they're gone." She laughs.

"I don't blame you. I love a good pizza," Chelsea says.

The pregame is on, and I see Casey's picture on the television, so they must be talking about him. Sometimes, I think about how surreal some of this life we're in is. He's on national television every week, and people know who he is. To me, he's just Casey—the guy who loves singing Taylor Swift songs with me, watching reality shows that have competitions, and eating sour candy—but to other sports fans, he's one of the best wide receivers in college football. Hard to wrap my head around it.

"Noelle, do you want my King jersey?" Charlie asks, noting the blue shirt I have on and not the jersey Casey bought me last year.

She looks down at her own jersey that has Beckham's number on it and then back at me. "I think Casey would be adamant that you should be wearing his name on your back today."

"I left it here, and it's somewhere in that mess of a room of his."

"You'll never find it in that closet. No worries. You can wear mine."

I follow Charlie to her and Beck's room. It's the only one that's been fully decorated, although the whole house looks much different, in a good way, than it did our freshman year.

When she moved in fully last year, she painted the walls in here pink, and there are peonies everywhere.

She walks into her closet and takes the jersey off the hanger, handing it to me. "Here you go. You can change in my bathroom."

"I'll just go into Casey's room." I nod my head toward the door. "Thank you for this. He texted twice today, asking for a selfie. We may have to take a pic and send it to him as proof of life that the jersey still exists." I laugh.

Charlie's smiling at me in a way that makes me think she knows more about what's really going on between me and Casey, aside from the situation with Trey. What started as a means to an end has become a beginning of sorts. A very sexy beginning.

"Gotta represent our guys—you know what I mean?" she says, following me out the door.

I laugh nervously. "Yep!"

When I get into Casey's room, I shut the door. I've been in here many times, but always when he's home. The difference now is that I'm looking at his space with *I want to smell his sheets and shirts* thoughts. That might be weird, but Casey has always smelled good to me. Now though, his clean, soapy smell is like a freaking aphrodisiac.

I take my time looking around his room. It's not a big space, so there isn't much to look at, but he does have pictures on his dresser. Most of them are with me, and he has some with just him and his sister, some with just Beck, one with Archie, Liam, and Beck, and then a picture of himself holding the championship trophy last year.

I wasn't able to go to that game, but I definitely watched. Seeing him so happy made me cry. I wish I could have been there with him to celebrate. We did when he got home though. I took him to his favorite Mexican restaurant, and we lived it up good. All the tacos and even dessert that night. Wild and crazy.

There's a T-shirt lying on the bed, and I can't help but pick it up. Holding it to my nose, I inhale, and it smells just like him. Which makes me smile and miss him like crazy. He's only been gone for a day, and it's not like I'm not used to him being gone. I guess it just feels different now.

What are you doing, Noelle?

Months ago, if someone had told me I'd be kissing Casey King, I would've laughed in their face. If they'd said he'd have his hand down my pants, giving me my first orgasm, I'd have spit out my drink. And yet here I am, going through the motions of this fake relationship. Kissing him at a drive-in. Going on real dates. Moaning his name on my couch. Acting like it's the most natural thing in the world. None of it has scared me. None of it has made me stop and think about what it might mean.

My phone buzzes in my pocket, and I pull it out, Casey's shirt still in my hand. It's a text message from an unknown number. I assume it's just another spam text, but when I open it, I nearly drop my phone.

> Unknown: Are you done ignoring me yet?

What the hell?

> Noelle: Who is this?

Pretty sure I know, but I ask anyway.

> Unknown: Stop playing games, Noelle. You know it's your favorite slugger.

Trey. I gag at his use of the nickname I called him when we first started dating. Back when I enjoyed being his girlfriend.

I keep blocking his calls. Does he get a new phone every time I block him, just to be able to text me? Or is he using someone else's phone?

> Noelle: Delete my number.

As soon as my message sends, another comes through before I can block this number too.

> Unknown: It's been five months, Noelle. I haven't been with another girl since you walked out of the apartment. I'm miserable without you. I miss you.

> Noelle: It's over, Trey.

> Unknown: Okay. You need more time. Don't make me wait too long. Like I told you before, you're mine.

I know I shouldn't entertain his texts. It's what he wants—a response. Yet, like I've always done in the past, I'm drawn into the drama and Trey's web of manipulation.

> Noelle: I'm with Casey now. The difference is, he actually respects me.

> Unknown: He'll be tired of you soon, and when he is, you'll come running back to me, like you always do.

> Noelle: You? The guy who cheated and made me feel like nothing?

> Unknown: You're so dramatic. We had our fights, but we were good together. You can't rewrite history, Noelle. You loved me.

I block the number and put my phone back in my pocket.

Hands trembling, I fold Casey's shirt and lay it back on the bed, then change my shirt to the jersey. After a few calming breaths, I give myself a shake. Even though it's not the first time he's texted from an unknown number, the fact that he's doing it again is a problem.

I take a minute to look at myself in the small mirror that hangs on his wall. For the first time in a long time, I see someone who doesn't look so unsure of herself, despite the unexpected text.

It's taken me a while to see it, but I changed with Trey. I was never overly confident before him, but I was pretty secure with myself. The longer I was with him, the less confident I became. And looking back, I think it all happened so gradually, like him making comments about my clothes. Then he would talk about my friends and make fun of them for various things.

I'll never forget, shortly after we had sex for the first time, how he talked about my stomach being soft and that it would be a good idea for me to cut calories and go to the gym regularly. Not really something you want to hear when you're already feeling a little vulnerable.

His behavior toward me seemed to change after that, too, like he was always irritated with me. Most of the time we were together, I felt like I was walking on eggshells, waiting to see what kind of mood he was in.

And when I asked him about it one time, he told me, "I don't have to work for you anymore. I got you."

When I left the room to take a shower, I cried. I just couldn't understand what I had done to make him want to hurt me that way. Then, when I came back into the room, he acted like nothing was wrong and asked me what I wanted to watch. I was so stunned and hurt. But in all honesty, that was just the beginning of how badly he treated me.

Even now, more memories pop up, and I think about why on earth I stayed with him for so long. But it's easy to make excuses for bad behavior when you think you're in love with someone.

And I also think if I hadn't had Casey in my life, it would have been a lot worse. It was like he balanced out the negative parts of Trey, so I didn't completely crumble.

"Noelle, the game is getting ready to start," Charlie yells from outside the room.

"Coming!" I pull out my elastic and redo my ponytail since it got a little messy when I changed and walk out of the room.

Chelsea is talking to Arbor on the couch, and they seem to be getting along well. Lily is next to Arbor, listening in on their conversation.

Charlie is sitting in one of the oversized chairs, and she pats the space next to her, wanting me to come sit with her. "Sit with me so we can cheer for our guys. I don't think these three have the same kind of interest as we do."

Arbor stops talking. "That's not true! I love watching the games. I just prefer to be there in person. I get bored, watching them on the television. I don't know how you do it."

"I love watching them play. What can I say? My boyfriend is not only hot, but he's insanely talented. And of course my brother is also amazing. Then, the other guys, I feel like they're all family, so I'm definitely invested." She pulls her legs over a little more to give me room to sit.

Arbor laughs and rolls her eyes, then goes back to talking to Chelsea and Lily.

On the television, the team is lined up at the opening of the tunnel. I can see Bo in the front, with Casey and Beck slightly behind him. Casey is rocking back and forth on his feet, and I can tell he's anxious to get out on the field. Some of the other guys are jumping up and down behind him, tapping his helmet.

The camera cuts in close, talking about Bo and his talent, but all I can see is Casey. He's got eye black on, and his eyes look intense, but he's wearing a slight smirk on his face. He really is so hot. It's crazy to me that he hasn't ever really had a girlfriend.

Charlie nudges me. "Hey, are you okay?"

I look at her and smile. "Yeah, totally." I decide not to say anything about Trey's text because I know she'll tell Casey.

I can feel her looking at me.

"Okay. If you're sure." She touches my arm.

"I'm good." I place my hand on hers.

"So ... you and Casey ..."

"Yeah?" I try to act nonchalant about it, but I know what she's asking me.

She chuckles. "Okay, so you're going to make me ask." She turns her body to look at me, but also possibly to shield the other girls from hearing us. "Are you sure you know what you're doing?"

"Well, I mean, what did he tell you?" I really hope he hasn't told her that I asked him to have sex with me. I would be mortified.

"Noelle, you know I like you, and we've always gotten along, but my brother is literally the other half of me. I just don't want to see him get hurt by this. I know he's a big boy, but you have to know how he feels about you." She turns toward me fully and takes a serious tone. "He would be so pissed at me for talking to you about this, but I just really want to understand what's happening."

I drop my head back and close my eyes.

"I know why you're doing it, but I want to know where your head is too. You and Casey ... make sense, so I'm not at all surprised that you would say he's your boyfriend, but tell me how you really feel about him. Do you really see him as just a friend, or is there potential for more? Because for him—and again, he would kill me for telling you—this is more."

Hearing her say that makes me smile. I'm also a little nervous to put my cards on the table. Because, honestly, I don't really know what to feel about all of it. And I'm not naive enough to think the physical part of this arrangement won't affect our relationship.

I pause to think about my words because I think it's important for her to not only hear me, but to see the sincerity on my face. "Charlie, you know I love Casey." I look at her, and she nods. "He's truly the best friend I've ever had. Yeah, it was natural for me to blurt out his name to Trey—because Casey has always been there for me in every way. But in the last few weeks, I've felt a shift. I don't know if it's always something that's been there, simmering, or what. But I want to be around him in a different way than I did before. Does that make sense? I'm not great at explaining this, but I want you to know I have no intention of hurting him."

Her expression, which was laced with concern, changes to one of relief, with a wide smile and big eyes. "So, are you thinking you want to see if this could turn into something real?"

"I honestly don't know what to think or feel right now. Things are definitely changing between us in more ways than one. I do know that he means everything to me, and I would never survive losing him as a friend." And I mean that.

"What are you two talking about over there?" Lily asks from her place on the couch.

Charlie looks at me before she speaks—asking permission, I think. "We're just talking about Casey and Noelle finally getting together."

Lily jumps up from the couch. "Wait, are you serious?"

I can't help but laugh. "I mean, we're testing the waters, I guess."

I know Charlie knows it started as a fake relationship, and the guys and these girls do know that Trey was bothering me, but they don't know that I told Trey we were dating. At least it doesn't appear that they know. So, even though I trust these girls, I think this is my chance to set the narrative. Because as much as I do like Lily, she's a talker.

"I literally couldn't be happier!" She claps.

"That's awesome, Noelle! I'm so happy you guys finally got your heads out of your asses." Arbor laughs.

"I honestly thought you were already dating on move-in day." Chelsea shrugs. "You guys are together, like, all the time. At least it seems that way when I'm home."

I suppose I have been really clueless.

"So, like, have you had sex yet?" Lily plops back down on the couch.

Charlie whips her head to Lily. "Lil, I don't think I need to hear about my brother's sex life."

"Oh hush, Char. Your poor brother has to live with you and Beck. We don't, and we still see you guys all over each other nonstop." She waves a hand at Charlie. "So, have you?"

I internally debate on how far I should take this conversation. I mean, I could talk to them about the sex lessons without telling them I asked for sex lessons. Because maybe there is something they could suggest to try? Fuck it.

"No, we haven't had sex yet. We're taking things a little slow." I shrug, and when I look at the girls on the couch, they're all looking at me like I'm insane. "What?"

"Noelle, respectfully, how much slower are you gonna take this? Foreplay has lasted, like, three years too long. The edging is intense, even from an outsider's perspective," Arbor says, which absolutely shocks me.

"I mean, she's not wrong. And, ladies, it's more like nine years. They met in middle school." Charlie cracks up. "Just no talk about body parts. Or if you do, give me a warning so I can plug my ears."

"Well, now that you mention it ..." Lily laughs. "Have you seen the peen?"

"Guyssss, seriously." Charlie plugs her ears and darts off to the kitchen.

I'm left with Chelsea, Arbor and Lily, each staring at me, waiting for information. I can feel that my face is red now by the heat in my cheeks, and while I know better than to divulge any intimate details about Casey, I realize how much I've missed this. The girl camaraderie. The sitting around and talking about guys.

"No, I have not," I tell them. "I'm not kidding when I say that we're taking it slow. We've really only kissed. And I've only been with Trey, so I don't feel like I know what I should be doing, if that makes sense. But for the record, I am very much looking forward to it."

"Well, I don't know what you're waiting for. Casey is fuck hot. I would be climbing that tree every chance I got." Lily purses her lips.

"Lily, seriously? You have a boyfriend." Arbor shakes her head.

"Don't tell me you don't think Casey's hot. I know you do because we've talked about it." Lily laughs, but my smile drops.

"I can think he's hot, but not want to bang him. He's like a brother to me." She looks at me. "Noelle, I have zero thoughts about Casey like that, but I do appreciate that he's a good-looking guy."

I release a breath I didn't realize I had been holding. "Oh, yeah, of course. And I agree; he's definitely hot. I guess what I'm trying to say is that I feel like I don't know what to do in bed. Trey just kind of took care of himself. There wasn't a whole lot of anything … else. You know what I mean?"

Lily nods. "I can totally see that with Trey. Selfish men are usually selfish lovers. But I don't see Casey being like that at all."

And based on what happened the other night, I can confirm he is not selfish.

"Lovers? Eww." Arbor laughs.

"What? It's true, and you know it." She points at Arbor.

"Well, I mean, no, I actually don't since I'm a virgin, but I can see Trey being that way for sure. He's a textbook narcissist." Arbor nods.

"Wait, you're still a virgin?" Chelsea chimes in.

"Yep. Not necessarily by choice, but it's just not been a priority. And don't get me wrong; my vibrator and I are well acquainted."

"Hey, are we done talking about my brother and sex?" Charlie asks, walking back into the room and removing her hands from her ears. "I want to watch the game today too."

"There's nothing really to tell, so we're good," Lily states.

"Great." She looks at me and smiles with a wink. "But seriously, I hope everything works out for you guys. I want nothing more than to see my brother as happy as I am."

"Thanks, Charlie. It's been a shift for sure, but, like, in a good way. For me at least. I don't know. I guess I'm also just trying not to overthink everything."

"Look, you know Casey doesn't play games, and he also doesn't do anything he doesn't want to do. So, when you are together, believe that he wants to be there. Just always be honest with him about what you're thinking and feeling." She wraps her arm around my shoulders and pulls me to her in a sideways hug.

I nod, feeling a little less awkward.

"Oh, I have an idea. Let's take a selfie, and I'll send it to Beck and Casey for them to see when the game is over. Casey will go crazy, seeing you in his jersey."

"Okay, he did ask for one earlier, but I agree, I think he'll like the jersey." I laugh, but also … it gives me butterflies to think that he will be happy to see me in his jersey again. Because it makes me happy to be wearing it.

CASEY

WE GOT HOME a few hours ago after winning our out-of-town game in New Orleans. I took a hit yesterday that didn't feel awesome. From my hip to mid-thigh, I have a beauty of a bruise. It's turning a gorgeous shade of purple already. But the touch-down I made, then coming into the locker room and seeing a text from my sister with Noelle sitting next to her, in my house and in my jersey, has distracted me from the pain. Because I can't stop looking at it.

She's the kind of pretty that doesn't beg for attention, yet turns every head in the room. Especially mine. The faintest freckles line her nose, her hair glistens in the sunlight, her mouth curves in this soft, knowing way, and her eyes … God, those eyes could talk me into anything.

I texted her when I got home, and she's on her way over now. It's my turn to go to the grocery store, so I asked if she would come with me.

I'm waiting by the window for her to pull up. I close out the picture of her and my sister and pull up Instagram. I go to my story and post the picture of them with the caption, *My two favorite girls.* I tag them both and share it.

Noelle's car stops at the curb in front of the house, and I don't wait for her to get out before I'm out the door to her car.

When I get into the passenger side, I lean in to kiss her. "Hi, pretty girl."

"Hi," she says softly against my lips and then angles herself back into her seat. "I'm glad you're back. You were awesome yesterday." She pulls away from the curb and starts driving.

"Thank you, and me too. I like sleeping in my own bed." I laugh. "So, you came over and watched the game here with the girls, huh? How did that go?" I ask because I'm curious if my sister said anything to her about us since I told her what was going on. But also, she hasn't spent much time with friends since school started, and as much as I want to monopolize her every free second, she needs to have genuine girl time.

"Yep. We had fun. Charlie and I were the only ones who really watched the game. Chelsea came with me and seemed to get along well with Lily and Arbor, so that was good. I think she's worse than I am about keeping herself busy. She's always working, so it was fun to hang out." She quickly glances over at me and smiles.

"That's awesome. She's welcome to come over anytime you come over. I like her, and she seems to be pretty drama-free."

Noelle only has one hand on the wheel, so I take her free hand in mine.

"Yeah, I really like living with her. It's just easy, you know?" She nods.

"So, you guys just sat around and talked, and you and Charlie watched the game, and then you went home?" I know I already asked, but she's not giving me much.

"Mmhmm. Well, your sister told them about us." She pulls into a parking spot and turns off the car, then turns to face me.

"She did, did she? What did she tell them?" I reach over and tuck a loose hair behind her ear, and she leans into my hand.

Her cheeks flush, and she shrugs. "She just told them that we were together. Not that it was fake."

Fake. The word feels wrong in my head. I don't want what we have to be an act, something temporary to toss away when it's served its purpose. I want it to be real—every look, every touch.

"And what did they say about us being together?" I brush my thumb over the top of her hand.

She laughs lightly. "Well, they said it was about time, then asked if we've had sex." She turns her head away from me when she says it.

"Sounds about right. Let me guess. Lily asked?" I chuckle.

"She sure did. But your sister didn't really want to hear about it, so the conversation was cut pretty short." She looks down. "Your sister had a lot of questions though when it came to our intentions. What exactly did you tell Charlie about us?"

I could go two ways with this. I could tell her that I told my sister that I'm head over ass in love with her and I'm gonna take this opportunity to make her realize we're good together. Or I could tell her what I think she's ready to hear right now.

When I search her face, I go with what I think she's ready for.

"I told her that Trey was bothering you and that you told him I was your boyfriend." Which is also the truth, just not all of it.

"And that's it?" She raises her brows.

"That's it. Why? Did she say something else to make you uncomfortable?" Because now I'm curious about what my sister told her. "I didn't tell her about the sex lessons. Is that what you mean?"

"No, I was just curious." She raises her voice slightly, like you do when you've been caught doing something you shouldn't have been and you're trying to deny it.

I search her face again, trying to figure out if I'm missing something. "Okaaay. Let's go get this done. I'm hungry, and then I want to crash."

I let go of her hand and get out of the car. When she rounds the hood, I take her hand in mine again, and we walk into the store.

We make our way through produce. A bulk of my list for the house is here so the cart is already getting full. Then we go to the butcher and grab a bunch of chicken breasts, some ground turkey, and a few steaks.

"I need to get my sister some more coffee, so let's go down this aisle." I steer the buggy down the row toward the coffee, but Noelle stops me.

"Case! Look, they have the cereal with the Christmas marsh-mallows already, but I only see one box." She's not that short, but she jumps up to try to reach it. When she does, she knocks the box to the back of the shelf. "Shit!"

"Let me see if I can get it." I'm a tall guy, so I should be able to grab it, but it's slid to the very back of the deep shelf. "Fuck. Okay, let's do this." I squat and hold up my arms. "Get on my shoulders."

She laughs. "Casey, I am not getting on your shoulders."

"Yes, you are if you want that cereal. Come on. Hop on." I take one of her hands and pull her closer.

She moves behind me, grabs my other hand to steady herself, then straddles my shoulders. "Oh God. Do not drop me, Casey King."

"As if I would ever. You ready?" I tilt my head to look at her.

"I'm ready." She squeezes my hands.

We both start laughing when I stand. I walk us closer to the shelf, and she leans forward to get the box.

"Urgh, I still can't get it. Can you turn to the side?"

So, I do.

"I got it!" She shakes the box in her hand.

When I turn us, we see her old roommate, Zoey, and some other girl I've never met standing at the end of the row. Noelle squeezes my hand she's holding.

"Oh, hey, Noelle." Zoey waves as if she didn't get caught fucking Trey. "How are you?"

I hear Noelle whisper, "You can't be serious."

I look at the other girl, and she's staring at me.

I look at the other girl and she's staring at me. "Don't I know you?" she asks.

"That's Casey King. He's on the football team," Zoey tells her.

"Right! I knew you looked familiar." The girl's smile widens.

I bend down low enough for Noelle to get off my shoulders. Once she's on the ground, I take her hand and pull her in close to me and wrap my arm around her waist. I still don't respond to either of their comments.

"Good game yesterday, Casey. That was an awesome catch," Zoey says.

And just to fuck with her, I say, "Oh, yeah? Which one?"

She stares at me, mouth open. "The one when you caught the ball …"

"In the first quarter?" I ask her.

Out of the corner of my eye, I see Noelle look up at me.

"Yes! That's the one." She smiles and nods.

"Yeah, that wasn't me." I look at Noelle. "You got what you wanted?"

She smirks at me, then looks over at Zoey. "Yep. I sure did."

As we pass them, I hear the girl I don't know ask Zoey if we're together. I don't wait to hear Zoey's reply because I really don't fucking care what she says. I never liked her, and then after what she did to Noelle … yeah, she can fuck right off.

I grab Charlie's coffee, and then we finish getting what I need and move toward the registers. We see Zoey and the nameless girl walking in the same direction, heads tilted toward each other, whispering, but I catch some of it.

"I thought it was a lie. Like, I didn't really believe Greer when she told us at the party at Trey's house yesterday, but I guess it's true. I wonder if Trey knows. Should I tell him?"

When we get to our line, I move Noelle in front of me and turn her so she's leaning against the bar of the buggy.

"What are you doing?" she asks, putting her hand on my chest.

"I just want to kiss my girlfriend," I say loud enough for the girls to hear me.

Noelle's eyes go wide. "Oh, okay—"

I don't let her finish. I keep one hand on the bar, and I wrap the other around her neck and pull her into me.

Our lips touch, and even though I kissed her in the car, I lose all sense of control right here in the middle of the grocery store. I tilt my head to deepen the kiss, and she lets me.

"Excuse me, sir. Are you checking out?"

We're interrupted by the cashier, who looks to be the same age as my grandma.

When I pull back from Noelle, her eyes are still closed, lips wet. I take my thumb and brush it across her bottom lip, then lean in again and kiss her one more time.

She opens her eyes this time when I pull back. "Wow," she whispers.

"Any day now, kids," the cashier says loudly.

Noelle and I both laugh.

"We'd better move. I feel like we're in trouble," she says, sliding her hand down to my stomach, making my muscles contract. She must feel it because she looks up at my face.

A throat clears next to us.

"Good to see you, Noelle!" Zoey chirps.

Noelle looks at her incredulously.

They walk away, and then I finish paying for my groceries.

After I get everything in the trunk, I get in the car, and Noelle is watching me.

"You good?" I ask her. I can't read the look on her face.

"Did you kiss me like that because you wanted to kiss me, or did you kiss me like that because they were there, watching?"

I take her hand in mine. "I kissed you because I absolutely wanted to. But it also served a purpose."

"What purpose?" she asks.

"It'll keep them talking, which will definitely get back to Trey." I wink at her. "Now, let's go home. I need to eat and sleep." I lean in and kiss her again because I really did want to kiss her in the store and I never want to think that any of this is for show.

CHAPTER
SIXTEEN

NOELLE

AFTER CASEY GOT to eat and I nibbled on a snack, we go back to his room to watch a movie. I don't intend on staying long tonight, but I don't really want to leave yet. I'm hoping we can have another lesson, but I know he's tired.

"Whatcha thinking about over there, pretty girl?" He rolls onto his side to face me.

Trey would have never been in tune with me enough to have any inkling that I was lost in thought. But also, he wouldn't have asked because he didn't care what I was thinking. And most of the time, I kept quiet because I didn't want to set him off.

I try not to make comparisons because Casey is a totally different person. It's just nice to have someone genuinely care about me.

Rolling to my side to face him, I decide I'm going to make the move tonight—the one I've been dreaming about for days and fantasized about while he was away.

I reach out and touch his face. His jaw, beautifully defined and strong, feels rough in my hand, as he's due for a shave.

"When the girls and I were watching your game, they had a

few questions about our relationship. Intimate questions." I poke out my tongue and slowly drag it over my upper lip. "I haven't been able to get the idea of something out of my head since. But I know you're tired, so we don't have to."

"Oh, yeah?" He smirks. "What have you been thinking about?"

I swallow down my nerves. "I want to see you."

His smile falls. "You want to see what exactly?"

"Casey, you know what I mean."

I drop my hand from his face, but he takes it in his hand and puts it back on his face and holds it there.

"Hey, it's me. You don't have to be shy or embarrassed. There is nothing you can ask that I won't do. I promise." He pulls my hand to his lips and kisses it.

"I don't know why I'm so nervous. It's you, and I don't want you to tease me for what I want from you." I can feel the heat hitting my cheeks and move my eyes from his.

"Noelle, look at me."

I comply.

"I would never ever tease you about something like this."

And I know that's true. "Okay, then I want you to take off your shirt first."

He drops my hand and sits up enough to remove his shirt. His shoulders are broad, tapering to a lean waist, and every muscle is defined like it was carved by intention. My eyes skim over the smooth plane of his chest before tracing over the ripples of his abs and the V that disappears beneath his shorts.

"What else?" He snaps me out of my trance that's following the dusting of hair running down the center of his torso.

"Will you take your shorts off?" I hear the lilt in my voice.

A smile spreads across his face. "I can, but I'm not wearing anything under them. You okay with that?"

Sweet Jesus. I mean, yes. Yes, I am.

"Yes," I manage to whisper.

Without taking his eyes off of mine, he lies back, tips his hips up, and slowly pushes his shorts off. When I see the head of his cock out of the corner of my eye, I can't help but look.

Just like every other part of him, his cock is absolutely perfect. Long and thick, vein running through the middle from base to head. I want to trace it with my tongue. Am I drooling?

As if it has a mind of its own, my hand reaches down, and I run my finger around the head. It twitches with my touch, and I'm mesmerized. I slide my hand down his length, but don't take ahold of it.

"Noelle," Casey breathes in.

I reach down between his legs and cup his balls. It shouldn't be sexy, but when Casey groans, I look up at his face. His head is tilted back, eyes closed.

"Does that feel good?" I ask him, genuinely wanting to know.

"Fuck yes." He opens his eyes and looks at me.

As I move my hand back up to his cock, I grab the base of it and lightly squeeze. He places his hand over mine and guides my hand up.

"Am I doing this right?"

It's not that I never touched Trey like this, but he just never let me touch him like *this*. He was always in a rush to get to sex. So, I feel like I missed out on a lot of foreplay. Including blow jobs. For some reason, he didn't really seem to like it, or I was just doing it wrong.

"Oh, yeah. You're doing so good." He licks his bottom lip.

Seeing his tongue peek out makes me want to kiss him. So, I do. I slide my tongue inside his mouth and twirl it around his slowly. Just like the movement of my hand, I want to memorize it all. I'm not in a rush.

His hips thrust up, and I take that as a signal to start moving my hand a little faster. So, I slide my hand up and down his length, and his hips move with it.

When I get to the tip again, I feel wetness, so I palm the head of his dick, coating my palm, then slide it back down, pumping.

He breaks our kiss. "Fuck, Noelle. You keep doing that, and I'm going to come pretty fast."

"Are you really?" I ask curiously. I probably sound stupid, but I'm kind of surprised I'm having this effect on him.

He nods. "Yep."

"Okay, well, before you do, I want to do something else." I don't let go of him, but I turn my body so I'm hovering over his dick.

I hear him mumble, "Oh shit."

My tongue swirls around the head, and then I wrap my lips around it and suck. It makes his hips thrust up, so I keep moving my hand up and down while taking him deeper into my mouth.

He places his hand on my head, but isn't pushing it.

When I reach the base of him, I hear him hiss, "So good."

His praise makes me feel more confident, so I continue moving my hand and mouth up and down his cock. I wish I could watch his face while I'm doing this. Maybe next time, I can. Because I do want there to be a next time.

"I'm getting close," he warns me, but I keep going.

I move the hand that I've had bracing me on the bed to his chest. He covers my hand with his just as I taste the first shots of cum hit my tongue. I don't stop. I keep taking him deep as he fills me.

When his hips stop moving, I release him, then wipe my mouth with my hand. With my other hand, I can still feel the rapid rise and fall of his chest.

"Holy hell. That was incredible." He runs his hand over my head, then down my back.

"Really?" I sit up and look at him. "I mean, I have done that before, but only a few times. Do you promise you would tell me if you didn't like it?"

He grabs his shorts and wipes himself off, then tosses them to the floor. Which means he's still lying naked. And I can't stop looking at his dick.

"Noelle, look at me. You were perfect. And if anyone ever

told you otherwise, they were lying." He chuckles. "Hell, I had to force myself not to come the second you put your hand on me. Better than a fucking fantasy."

"What do you mean? Have you ever thought about me doing that to you?"

He sits up, and he's right in my face.

"All the fucking time." He smirks and slides his hand around the back of my neck. "Kiss me."

He's fantasized about me giving him a blow job. Me.

I give myself a mental high five. And then I lean in and kiss him.

When he pulls back, he places a kiss on my forehead. "Thank you for that, truly. I wasn't expecting that, but it's like my birthday came early."

He laughs again, and I push him back onto the pillows.

"Are you spending the night?" he asks me, pulling me down to lie on his chest.

"I didn't really plan to, but if you want me to, I will. I just need to get up early so I can go home and shower and grab my stuff."

I trace patterns on his bare stomach. It's rock hard, but his skin is so soft.

His hand strokes my arm, giving me goose bumps. "I would really love it if you spent the night. And I would really love it if you let me return the favor."

"I mean, I wouldn't say no, but I know you're tired." I move my hand from his stomach back down to his growing erection.

"I'd never be too tired to make you come." He rolls us so I'm on my back and he's hovering over me. "You gonna let me taste your pussy tonight?" He bends his head and kisses me.

As we kiss, his hand moves under my shirt and up to my breast. We've established that he can make me come by playing with my breasts while fingering me, but I want more.

I break our kiss and move my hands to the bottom of my

shirt. When he sees what I'm doing, he uses his free hand to help me remove it. Then I sit up slightly and unhook my bra.

"Goddamn," he whispers. Then he leans down and takes a nipple into his mouth, then releases it with a pop. "You're perfect—you know that?"

I don't answer, but instead reach for the button on my jeans and unbutton them. I lift my hips and start to pull them down, but he sits up and replaces my hands with his, pulling my jeans, along with my underwear, down my legs.

As he moves back to me, he runs his hands from my thighs all the way up to my breasts. "Is this real?" he asks, eyes roaming my body.

I place my hands on his shoulders. "Oh, yeah. This is real. I want you inside me. I want it all."

"Noelle, we have time. We don't have to have sex tonight. I want you to experience everything so you know what you like and what you don't."

He leans back down to kiss me, his body to the side of mine. I can feel his erection against my thigh.

We kiss for what seems like forever, hands roaming over each other's body. I reach for his cock and start to stroke it.

He pulls his hips back and breaks our kiss. "Your turn."

With his eyes on mine, he moves down my body and between my legs, peppering kisses all the way down. I open my legs wider so he can lie between them.

"Look at you. Did sucking my dick make you wet?"

He doesn't wait for me to answer. Not that I could if I wanted to. Sexy Casey is a different Casey from the one I know. Not in a bad way. In a very good, fuck-me-into-the-mattress way.

At the first stroke of his tongue on my clit, my hips start to rise, but he puts his hand above my mound, holding me in place, restricting my movement. His other hand wraps around my thigh, holding my legs open.

This is definitely not something I've experienced before. My body feels like it's on fire every time he swirls his tongue.

"Casey, please let me move."

He doesn't answer and continues licking and sucking. Then he releases my leg and slides one finger inside of me while circling my clit with his tongue. His other hand moves from my mound, and he uses his fingers to keep me open to him.

I can feel it all. Every lick. Every stroke. Every thrust of his fingers.

"Come for me, pretty girl." He licks. "Give me everything." He sucks on my clit. "Let me taste that sugar on my tongue."

White-hot heat runs through my body as my orgasm hits, and I feel like I can't breathe from the intensity of it. But I finally move my hips, grinding against his face as my orgasm goes on and on.

Casey keeps going until I stop moving my hips. When I do, he kisses his way back up my body, then lies at my side. I turn my head to look at him, and when our eyes meet, we both smile.

"I have no words," I mumble because that's about all I can manage to get out.

He brings his hand to my face and cups my cheek. I lean into his touch. "You don't have to say anything. I can read it on your face." He brushes his thumb across my bottom lip. "My new favorite thing to do is make you come. And I'm gonna do just that every chance you give me."

"I guess you'd better get used to being on your knees then." Oh my God. Did I really say that out loud? He's made me lose all sense. "You're like the vagina whisperer." And now I can't stop talking. "I've literally never had an orgasm, and yet we've only been together like this twice, and you've completely comatosed me. I'm just sayin', a girl could get used to this."

"As you should. And I intend to be on my knees for you, always." He leans in and kisses me, and I can taste myself on his tongue. Another first.

It's a strange thing, not being a virgin, but also not experiencing a lot sexually. But I am glad I can share some firsts with my best friend. Because I feel like these are the moments I'll never forget.

CHAPTER
SEVENTEEN

CASEY

WE'RE PLAYING KANSAS TODAY, which is one of our biggest games of the season. I'm playing like shit, and we're down by ten points after the first half. I dropped a pass, then another got intercepted. I feel like I'm fumbling over my feet in every play.

It's halftime, and as I step into the locker room, Coach Pettys grabs a fistful of my jersey at the collar and yanks me toward the wall. The guys trail in behind me, slamming helmet crowns into lockers, kicking benches, and cursing Kansas. I glance at Coach, and the look he's giving me says I'm about to get lit up.

"King," he barks, "you've had balls hit you in the hands today—routine grabs—and you're letting 'em hit the grass. If I didn't know better, I'd think your head was somewhere else, not reading the coverage."

"No, sir. I'm locked in. They're pressing me at the line, rolling that safety over the top. Their DB's been all over me all game—hard to shake loose."

"I don't care if they're running man, bracket, or triple coverage. You've got to find separation. We've got a lot of young guys in this locker room—talented guys—who'd jump at the chance to run your routes. I'll be damned if I let you lose your spot because you're too busy scanning the bleachers instead of the secondary."

I shake my head, pissed at myself because he's right. Football is my life. I run every route like it's the game winner, give one hundred and ten percent on every snap. But I'd be lying if I said I hadn't stolen a look at the stands, looking for a certain brunette wearing my number.

"I'm your guy, Coach. I'll make the plays."

"Good. Because the morale's tanking out there. We need a momentum shift, and it starts with you. Move the chains, get the sideline fired up. You with me, King?"

"I'm with you, Coach." He releases me and I go sit at my locker and hang my helmet on a hook.

Beck drops onto the bench beside me, helmet in his lap, sweat dripping off his face. A towel hangs around his neck while our trainer retapes both his wrists. He's been getting cooked all game. Every snap, he's taken a shot.

Coach gives a loud whistle, silencing the room, and lays into us about our miserable performance. I can't say the guy is wrong. We listen as he gets fired up, gets us fired up, and gets louder as his speech gets longer.

"Now, it's time to get your fucking heads out of your asses and win this game! No more mistakes. No more excuses. Refocus. Show them why you're the national fucking champions. Let's go!" He walks out of the locker room.

Bo, also bandaged, steps into the center of the room. "As your leader, my job is pretty fucking clear to me. It's my duty to get out on that field and play the best I can regardless of who is on the field with me. I believe in all of you. I know you can push yourself to the absolute limit because I've fucking seen it. I know we have the ability and the mental fortitude to get out there and win this thing! We have a job to do. Now let's go fucking do it!" He claps, then raises his arm. "Come and gather up."

We all stand and form a circle around him.

"Stallions on three. One! Two! Three!"

"Stallions!" the team chants.

I go back to my stall and grab my helmet, and we all file out. No one is saying much as we walk through the tunnel.

When I get to the bench, I see my family and Noelle sitting near the front row again. Noelle gives me a slight wave, and I lift my chin and give her a smile.

Kansas's offense is on the field, but I stand on the sideline to watch what's happening. Bo's and Coach's speeches must have worked because our defense is stopping every play.

With my helmet in hand, I walk out on the field and into the huddle. Bo is checking his wristband, looking at the play calls. Beck is at my side, and I look at him and nod. A silent signal asking if he's okay. He nods back.

"Okay, guys, let's get back in this game. Red weak, power right. Break."

We all clap once and line up in our formation for this play. Beck will run the ball, aiming for the first down. With our field position right now, if he can at least get the first down, it'll get us where we need to be to score with the next play.

Bo calls the snap, and I take off running, moving around my defender, in the off chance that Bo needs to throw me the ball. When I look to the right of the field though, I see Beck has the ball tucked in his arm, plowing through the defenders on the right side. Despite his double coverage, he makes the first down.

When we get back into the huddle, Bo calls the next play. "You're a beast, Linson. Good run." He taps Beck on the helmet. "Red strong, left sixty-three, Ohio. Break."

We all clap once.

With this play, I'll run a straight route toward the end zone, and Bo will pass the ball to me. When Bo snaps, I take off and juke to the left to move around the cornerback and give myself enough room to catch the ball while also staying in bounds. I turn to my right side and see the ball flying through the air toward me. It's a beauty of a throw, and there's no way in hell I'm not catching this pass.

I've positioned myself in the line of fire, and the ball is close enough to me that I can see the spiral. I reach up and grab the ball in both hands, then tuck it into my right side since the cornerback is on my heels on my left, dig my foot in, and run straight to the end zone.

My teammates meet me there and smack my helmet, congratulating me on the score. I toss the ball to the ref, then run back to the sideline. As I run, I look to the stands and see everyone who is important to me on their feet, clapping, and Charlie and Noelle are jumping up and down.

I can't help the stupid smile that spreads across my face. Because this day, the game, just turned around.

We won the game by a touchdown that Beck ran in. Thank God because, with the way we played tonight, we're already gonna have hell this week at practice. At least now, we may not have to do two-a-days.

I've showered, and I'm getting dressed by my locker when Silas walks over to me.

"Good game, King. You going to that neon-party thing at Smith's tonight?"

"I don't know. Maybe. You going?" I look at him.

"Yeah, should be a fun time. Not sure I've ever been to one though. Do I just wear white or what?" He shakes out his still-wet hair and it hits me in the face.

"Dude, I just put my shirt on, and now I'm wet again." I shove him.

He laughs. "Sorry, man. At least I showered. Could've been worse—you feel me?" His brow rises, and he puts his fist out for a bump.

I ignore him, but laugh. Then I grab my phone from the top shelf of the locker. "Let me just see what the plan is tonight."

Since the night of the best blow job of my life, Noelle and I have spent nearly every free minute together. We haven't had sex yet, but I have no doubt it's coming soon—and not because we haven't wanted to, but really, I just want to make sure this is heading in a direction that's permanent. I think it is. I hope it is. But we're also having fun, messing around. She's not as naive in the bedroom as she thought she was. And I'm definitely reaping the benefits of her exploration. Trey was just a selfish asshole. She knows exactly what she's doing.

I don't see a text from her yet, so I shoot one off, asking what she wants to do tonight. As I wait, I see a notification from Instagram from her. It's a carousel of pictures from the game. One of her and my sister in the stands. They're wearing their jerseys, but also little stickers or something on their faces with my and Beck's numbers. She looks so fucking cute. The other pictures are of me on the sidelines, one of my touchdown, and then of me running off the field and waving to her. She must have posted these while I was in the shower.

But it's the caption that gets me—*My favorite story is ours.*

I mean, I'm no relationship expert, but that seems pretty real. I heart the post and make a comment—*My one and only*—which isn't fake either. She's the only girl I've ever loved. As I shoot it off into my story, my phone buzzes.

> Noelle: Up to you. Did you not want to go to the party?

> Casey: We can if you want. Is my sister going?

> Noelle: Yeah, I think she and Beck are going, and then some of her friends are meeting us there.

Casey: Okay then, let's do it.

> Noelle: I'm excited! I haven't been to a party yet this year.

Casey: Should be fun. Are you going home or to my house?

> Noelle: Your sister and I just left. I'm sorry we didn't wait, but we were going to run by my place so I could grab a white T-shirt and shorts.

Casey: Okay, I'll meet you at mine.

> Noelle: *kiss emoji*

I look over my shoulder and yell to Silas, "We're going. You want to walk over with us, or you going solo?"

Beck walks up to his stall. "Where are you going?"

"We're"—I motion between us—"going to Smith and Schuster's for that neon party they have planned tonight."

He points to himself. "I am?"

"Yes, according to Noelle. She and Charlie are stopping at her place to get some clothes, and then they're meeting us at the house."

My phone dings with another notification.

I pull it up and see Noelle has hearted my comment, then below it, my sister commented—*Love this for you guys!*

I smile and shake my head, then pocket my phone.

"Fuck. Okay." When he bends over to reach into his locker, he winces.

"You good?" I ask him.

"Yeah, I'll be fine. I'm gonna have a good bruise over the next few days though." He turns, and I see a deep bruise forming that stretches from just below his ribs around to the back.

"Fuck, man. You get Sally to look at that yet?" I ask him as I grab my bag. Sally is our head team trainer. She keeps us all patched up and healthy.

"Yeah, she looked at it before I got in the shower. No broken ribs, so just a deep tissue bruise. I'll be fine. I'll ice it later. And I'm sure your sister will take good care of me." He winks at me, trying to get a rise out of me.

"Fuck off." I laugh and shove his shoulder. "You riding with me or Bo?"

"You can go if you don't want to wait, but I'll be ready in a few minutes. I don't even see Bo back here yet. He must still be in the press room." He dresses quickly, then grabs his bag and phone. "See, ready." He chuckles.

"Let's roll. Silas, you coming or what?" I yell over to him.

He does a handshake with Smith, then heads in our direction. "All right, boys, let's go. I need to get ready. I plan to get laid tonight." He holds a hand up for a high five, but Beck and I just shake our heads and laugh. "Leavin' me hangin'. Not cool."

"Let's move, Casanova. My girl is waiting for me," Beck says dryly.

"King?" He holds his hand out to me.

This is the first time he's ever really talked about hooking up with girls. I mean, I'm sure he does, but he's been kind of the quiet guy in the house so far.

"You do what you need to do, buddy." I pat his shoulder. "But like he said"—I point my thumb at Beck—"I need to get home to see my girl."

"Pussy-whipped. Both of you," he mumbles.

I can't help but smile because, yep, I sure am. And we haven't even had sex yet.

CHAPTER
EIGHTEEN

NOELLE

EVEN THOUGH WE'VE been doing the whole fake-dating thing for a while now, tonight, we're going to our first party as a couple. Travis Schuster and Dan Smith live there, and they are a little … wild. I'm honestly surprised that they haven't gotten in trouble with the coach yet. Some of their parties have gotten pretty crazy.

Tonight, they're having a neon party, so I'm guessing that means there will be paint and black lights, but who knows with these guys? They might mean that everyone should wear neon clothes. Guess we'll find out soon enough.

When Charlie and I pull up to their house, Casey's truck is already in the driveway. I can't help the butterflies in my stomach at the thought of seeing him, and I feel like I can't get out of the car fast enough.

Weird thing is, Casey and I have always been close, but adding in the sexy stuff is making me feel even more connected to him. I think about him when we're not together. I'm the happiest I've ever been when we are together. And experiencing new things sexually has been mind-blowing.

I know he's been wanting to give me time and take things slow, but I'm starting to run out of patience. Not that I'm not taking full advantage of what we have been doing, but I'm ready. I want to feel completely connected to him.

Charlie walks in ahead of me and shouts, "Honey, I'm home!"

Beck is sitting on the chair in the family room as we walk in the front door, so when she walks by him, he grabs her around the waist and pulls her into his lap. The kiss they share is slightly obscene, but also ... kinda hot. They have that kind of electric chemistry that you can't help but admire.

Casey comes from the hallway, so he must have been in his room. He's wearing jeans and a white T-shirt. I'm not sure what it is about guys in white T-shirts, but he looks so freaking fine.

"Hey." He lifts me in his arms when he reaches me, making me drop the bag in my hand with my clothes to change into for the party.

"Hello, Casey King." I can't help but giggle.

Even though we've moved into a different dynamic of our relationship, I don't want anything about what we've had to change.

He kisses me hard, then lowers me back to the ground. "Hello, Noelle James." Bending slightly, he kisses me again. "You need to change so we can go." He nods to the bag next to my feet.

"Okay, okay. And we're sure this is, like, a paint, black-light type of neon party and not a '90s type of neon party?"

I pick up my bag and start to walk toward his bedroom. He smacks my ass as I walk by him.

"I mean, who knows for sure? But apparently, there is paint involved." He starts walking in the other direction toward the kitchen. "I'll be in there in a second. I'm just gonna get a water. You want one?"

"Yes, please," I call over my shoulder.

When I get to his room, I set the bag on the bed, take off my coat, and pull out the short shorts and the crop top that Charlie talked me into wearing. I don't usually dress like this, but I figured I didn't really want to ruin any of my clothes that I actually wear.

Casey walks in and hands me a water bottle. I open it and take a sip, then close it and set it on the dresser behind me.

"Do you need help getting dressed?" He turns and closes the door. "I'm happy to be of assistance." His hands slide around my waist, and he pulls me into him.

I wrap my arms around his neck, tilt my head up, and kiss him first, teasing my tongue along his top lip, making him groan. One of my hands slides up the back of his head, and I pull him into me further to deepen the kiss. Our tongues move together slowly. Sensually. And I'm ready to forget this party and climb onto that bed instead.

He must read my mind because he pulls back and says, "We don't have to go to the party. We can stay right here all night." He kisses me again, not waiting for an answer, and takes the bottom of my shirt and starts to pull it up.

I break the kiss so he can pull my shirt off. "I mean … it's not a terrible idea." My hands hook into the waistband of his jeans, and I tug. "What do you think? Stay or go?"

"Casey, let's go!" Charlie knocks and yells from outside the door.

"Cockblocker," he mumbles. "Give us five. Noelle is changing."

"So, we're gonna go?" I ask, torn between staying and going, more out of curiosity than anything.

"Yeah, let's go for a little while, and then we can come back here later and finish this." He places my hand on his cock.

"Promise?" I take his hand and put it between my legs.

"Fuck, pretty girl. I can feel your heat through your jeans. Are you wet for me?" He unbuttons my jeans and slides his hand inside my panties. "Goddamn."

"Casey," I moan.

Another knock, this one is harder.

"Yo! King! Let's roll." This time, it's Silas.

Casey leans his forehead against mine. "Okay, let's get this over with." Then he pulls out his hand and traces my bottom lip with his fingers that were just in my underwear. He leans in and sucks my bottom lip into his mouth. "Sugar."

I'm melting. Literally.

"Okay, let's move. Do you want me to help you get dressed?" He wiggles his eyebrows, making me laugh.

"No! Because if you do, we definitely won't leave."

I shove him away from me, and he lands on his bed.

I change quickly, but once I'm dressed, I start to second-guess my outfit—mainly the white crop top that shows my stomach and, if I lift my arms, possibly the underside of my bra. Trey didn't like when I showed any kind of skin, and I wonder if Casey feels the same.

"What do you think? Is this okay?"

"Of course it is. Half the people there will probably end up in their boxers and shit. You look amazing, as always." He grabs my hips and pulls me toward him on the bed.

"Okay, but you think it's okay for me to wear a crop top?" I rub my bare stomach with one hand.

He looks at me for a minute, then moves my hand and places kisses on my stomach. When he pulls back, he asks, "Is this about Trey?"

"No! I mean, not about him, but he didn't like me wearing clothes that showed too much skin because he thought my stomach was too soft, so I just wanted to make sure you were okay with it." I place my hands on his shoulders.

Casey hangs his head for a minute and sighs. Then he kisses my stomach again before speaking. "Noelle, we're in a fifty-fifty relationship here. You can *dress* however you want." He pauses. "And I'll *undress* you whenever I want. But only because I want to see you naked and not because I have a say in what you wear. Come here."

He stands and takes my hand and moves us so we're in front of the mirror on his wall. My back is to his chest.

"What are you doing?" I release his hand and cover my bare stomach with my hands.

"Tell me what you see when you look in the mirror." He covers my hands with his.

"I don't know. What do you mean?"

"What do you see when you look at yourself?" He rests his chin on my shoulder.

"I see my plain brown hair, hazel eyes, freckles on my nose that I wish I could cover, boobs that are a little too small, and a tummy that would probably benefit from some sit-ups." I look at each body part while I speak.

"Do you want to know what I see?" He moves my hair to one side so he can kiss my neck.

"What do you see?" I breathe.

"I see beautiful brown hair with natural golden highlights that catch the sun. I see hazel eyes that I get lost in every time we make eye contact. I see freckles so cute that I want to kiss every single one. I see breasts that fit perfectly in my hands." His hands cup me. "And I see a stomach so silky smooth that I could kiss it and run my tongue across it all fucking day"—his fingertips graze my skin, setting it on fire—"and then all the way down to devour that perfect pussy of yours."

His fingers dip inside my shorts, and he circles my clit, no doubt finding me even wetter than I was before.

"Wear whatever you want, but don't wear it for me. Wear it because you feel good in it. Because to me, you're perfect, no matter what you have on. Although I prefer you naked."

Why are we going to this party again?

I mean, seriously, how did I get so lucky with this guy? And the best part about it all is, I know he means what he says because he shows me every day with his actions.

When we get to Smith and Schuster's house, there's a line out the door. Beck is not about to wait in line to get in since Charlie and I both don't have coats, so he plows us through. Which really just puts us right in the center of another crowd. I haven't been to many of the parties here, but it's definitely the most packed I've ever seen it.

The house is lit by black lights alone, and there are glow sticks everywhere. When we move toward the kitchen through the crowd, we see big sheets hanging around the room and people taking turns painting them with neon paint. I see one girl rub paint on her breasts, thankfully over her shirt, and press them against the sheet. Classy.

In the kitchen, there are bins with glow sticks to make bracelets, necklaces, and headbands. Charlie and I take a few of the sticks and start piecing them together.

"I feel like we're at a middle school dance or something." I laugh.

"Yeah, but with booze and naked bodies." She throws her head back and laughs.

"Okay, this one is ready. Come here, baby. Let me put this on your neck." She reaches for Beck, who opted not to wear white, and pulls his head back.

"Nope. That's all you, Boss." He takes her hand and kisses it.

"Beck, don't be a party pooper." She pouts.

"You're lucky you got me here at all. I was ready to—"

Charlie covers his mouth before he can finish speaking. "Beckham Linson."

She moves her hand, but he takes it and pulls her into him. He whispers something in her ear that makes her laugh.

Casey is standing next to me, putting his own stick jewelry together. He's already got a bracelet on, and it looks like he's making a necklace. "What do you think?" he asks as he finishes.

"You did so good!" I squeeze his biceps. "Here, help me put mine on."

I hand him my necklace, and he fastens it for me, then kisses the back of my neck.

"Do you want something to drink?"

He takes my hand, and we walk over to the counter with various bottles of alcohol and a small keg. My guess is that there is a bigger keg outside.

"Yeah, I'll just have a beer though. I'm not really in the mood to drink much." I don't drink much anyway.

He grabs two red cups from the stack next to the keg.

As he fills them, Dan Smith walks in and sees us. "What's up, fuckers?!" He's clearly been drinking already. Likely since they got home from their game. "Did you guys see the photo booth we got? It's in the dining room. You gotta try it!" He walks by Beck on his way out of the room and pats him on the shoulder. "Glad to see you dressed for the occasion, Linson."

Beck just shakes his head, but smiles.

"Let's go paint!" Charlie takes Beck's hand, and they walk out of the kitchen toward the paints.

"What do you want to do, pretty girl? Do you want to go paint, or should we check out that photo booth?" He leans in to kiss me.

"Let's go do the photo booth!" I shout over the music. "That sounds fun. I don't think we have any photo booth pics. Do we?"

I take his hand and lead him into the dining room, where the booth is set up. There's another couple in there now, and we see their pictures drop outside the booth. They're covered in paint by the looks of it. I wonder if Smith and Schuster paid a deposit for the booth—because they're most definitely losing it if it's covered in paint.

As soon as they walk out, we hear Schuster on a megaphone, announcing a painting contest, encouraging everyone to "be creative." I'm terrified to know what he means by that.

I look at Casey, and we both laugh.

"Come on. Let's do this while there's no line." He pulls me into the booth and closes the curtain.

We sit on the small bench seat and get centered in the frame. He hits the Start button for the camera, and the timer counts down from five.

"Okay, are we going funny or serious?" He puts his forefinger and thumb on his chin and purses his lips at the screen, and I can't help but laugh.

"Umm … I think we should just be us."

I turn my body toward his and drape my legs over his. Then I wrap my arms around his neck and pull him into me for a kiss. I feel his arm stretch out and then hear the clicking sounds of the camera.

We don't stop kissing, even after the clicking stops. My hands are in his hair, and his palms are sliding up and down my back, stopping at the top of my jeans and then up again.

He reaches around to the front of my shirt and slides a hand under my crop top. With skilled hands, he pulls down one cup of my bra. The idea of being exposed like this, with people on the other side of the curtain, is giving me an adrenaline rush.

When he pinches my nipple, I gasp.

"More." I suck his bottom lip into my mouth, and he groans and does it again.

He breaks our kiss and I pout, lips pursed, as he pulls me onto his lap, my back to his front.

"Open for me," he demands.

My legs are draped over his thighs, so when he spreads his legs, my legs open wider in unison. He brushes my hair to the side, leaving my neck exposed in the way he knows I love. I watch the screen in front of us, the one that's dark and reflective of us, and become captivated by the sight of Casey as he licks and sucks on my neck while his hands cup my breasts—kneading and twerking them in a way he's become expert in in such a short time. I lean my head back on his shoulder to give him more access to my neck.

"Casey," I pant.

"We have to be quiet. Can you do that for me?"

He sucks hard on the side of my neck and pulls one of my nipples. Lightning shoots through me at the sensation.

"Yesss. I can." My hands reach behind me and around his neck, making my chest completely open to him.

One hand continues to pinch and pull my nipple while his other hand moves down my stomach and into my shorts. At the first swipe of his finger through my center, I have to bite down on my lip to stay quiet. I know there is a lot of noise out there right now, but I would die if someone walked by and figured out what we were doing in here.

"I'm gonna make you come. I want that tight pussy squeezing my fingers. I want you to feel every. Single. Stroke. Can you come for me?" His fingers move in circles over my clit.

"Yes," I say, turning my head to reach his mouth for a kiss. It's wet and messy. And I've never been more turned on.

He sucks on my tongue and releases it, then moves his mouth to my ear. "Good girl." As he says it, his fingers enter me and hit a spot that makes me see stars. "That's it. Roll your hips."

My hips are circling in as he pumps his fingers in and out of me, and I feel like I'm on the edge of reaching my orgasm. I can feel his hard cock between my ass cheeks, which just turns me on even more. Knowing he's hard because he's getting me off makes me lose control.

"Casey, I'm gonna come," I pant.

I feel him stretch his legs out, which opens my legs further. His thumb is circling my clit while his fingers move in and out.

"That's it. You look so beautiful, spread out for me like this.

Let me feel you come." As he says it, his other hand pinches my nipple hard.

My head drops back, and my mouth opens, but no sound comes out as wave after wave of my orgasm rolls through me.

"Casey," I breathe. "Feels so good." I turn my head and kiss the side of his neck as I come down.

"Come here." He turns his head and cups my face with his hand. "You are everything. Believe me when I tell you, you are everything."

He kisses me softly, and I melt into him.

As I come out of my orgasm haze, I realize we've probably been in here for a while.

"We should get out there, huh? Other people might want to use this." I can feel my face flush at the thought of what we just did in here.

"Yeah, I guess we should." He lifts me off of his lap, then adjusts his hard-on. "Let's grab our pictures and see what came out."

After adjusting my clothes, we open the curtain and take our pictures from the drop slot. The first set of three are of us kissing, and I absolutely love them. The second set, which I didn't realize we took, is of us … doing what we just did. Luckily, nothing is really showing, but the looks on our faces make it pretty clear what was happening.

In one of them, Casey's looking directly at the camera, his eyes intense. The second one, his face is tucked into my neck, and his tongue is touching my skin. The last one, my head is on his shoulder, my mouth is open, and Casey's looking down, which tells me he was probably watching what he was doing. Front-row seat really. Between what was probably the reflection in the glass and being able to see his hand moving in and out of me … yeah, I'm kind of jealous actually.

Casey's looking over my shoulder, and I hear him suck in a breath. "Holy fuck, those are hot."

"Yeah," I whisper. "I didn't realize you took more pictures."

"Are you mad?" He places a kiss behind my ear.

I turn my head to look at him. "Uh, no. These are amazing. I just didn't realize you were doing that."

"Well, you were a little preoccupied." He wraps his arms around my waist and tugs me back into him.

"Hell yeah, I was." We both laugh. "Okay, but what are we gonna do with these? I can't carry them around all night, and I don't have pockets in these shorts."

He plucks them out of my hand and puts them in his back pocket. "Problem solved. Now let's go pretend to be artists."

With my hand tucked in his, we walk into what should be the family room area, and I stop walking when I see Trey across the room. Of course, he sees me too. His attention becomes rigid, and there's a weird smirk that appears on his face.

"Shit." I tug on Casey's hand.

"What's wrong?" He tilts his head toward me to hear me better since it's loud in the room.

"Trey is here." I nod toward the other side of the room, where Trey is looking our way.

Casey lifts his chin, and his jaw tightens at the sight of my ex-boyfriend.

"Fucking asshole. He's got balls, showing up here."

He starts to pull me farther into the room, but I pull back, to little effect.

"What are you doing? He's gonna see us."

"And? Wasn't that the point at the start of all this anyway? Now he can see it and just not hear about it." He looks down and smirks at me. Like he thinks this is funny.

"Casey, wait. Seriously, let's just go somewhere else in the house." I try to pull on his hand, but he holds our hands in place.

"Noelle"—he tips my chin up so I'm looking at him—"I'm not afraid of Trey. I'll walk right up to him and shake his hand with the same hand that just made you come." He's looking into my eyes with complete seriousness.

I swallow. "Okay, but why is that so hot?" I say quietly, but loud enough for him to hear me.

"You want me to claim you, pretty girl? Right here? Right now? In front of all these people?" A smile grows on his face. "Just so there's no confusion or doubting what we are."

"What are we?" I ask him, reaching up and holding his face.

He leans in to kiss me. "I am yours, and you are mine. That's what we are."

His words make me forget that anyone else is in the room, and I wind my arms around his neck and attack his mouth. His arms wrap around my waist and pull me into him so it's like we're melting together.

When I pull back, I look into his eyes, and we both smile.

"Hey, there you guys are!" Charlie bounces over to us. "You have to see what Beck and I painted! It's electric!" She throws her head back and laughs.

When Casey takes my hand in his and we follow, I can't help but look over to where Trey was, but he's gone. And I couldn't be more relieved.

CHAPTER
NINETEEN

CASEY

MY SISTER and my best friend—otherwise known as Picasso—thought they'd created some kind of masterpiece, but I had no idea what I was looking at. I mean, I think there was a little stick figure in the corner.

Noelle and I took the paint experience by the hand. Literally. We painted each other's skin and clothes. So, between the game win, photo booth, and the paint, it's been a great fucking night.

We just got back to my house, which was a short walk from the party, and I'm ready to get my girl in bed. But first, we need a shower. With her hand in mine, we walk to my room, and I grab two towels from the closet. Then I take our pictures from my pocket and set them on the dresser.

"You aren't going to leave those out are you?" She asks, with a nervous laugh.

"Of course not. I'll keep them somewhere safe for just us to look at from time to time." I lift her hand and kiss it. "Shower with me?" I look at her with a smirk, brow raised in question.

She smiles shyly and nods.

When we walk in, I place the towels on the towel rack, lock

the door, then turn on the water. Silas is still at the party, and I'm not really sure where Bo was tonight, but to be safe, I don't want either of them walking in on us.

I turn back to Noelle, and she's already pulling her shirt off. Because it's a crop top, her stomach is pretty much covered in paint, and my handprints are on the cups of her bra. Does it make me smile? Abso-fucking-lutely.

"What are you smiling at?" she asks as she unhooks her bra.

"I like seeing my handprints on you." I reach behind me and grab the back of the neck of my shirt and pull it over my head, then toss it to the floor next to hers.

She's unbuttoning her shorts slowly, watching me as she does. Once she slides them off her legs, she lifts them and turns them around. "So then, you like these handprints too?"

My palms are perfectly placed on the shorts pockets. And, yes, I like that too.

"Hell yeah, I do."

I quickly unbutton my jeans and push them and my boxers down my legs and kick them into the corner. Then I reach for her and wrap my hands around her to take hold of her ass. It's perfect. With our height difference, my dick hits her stomach, so I lift her up and set her on the counter between the two sinks.

"I thought we were getting in the shower." She smirks.

"Oh, we will. But first, I need a taste." I drop down to my knees in front of her and push her thighs apart so she's completely open to me. "Fuck, that's a pretty pussy." Leaning closer, I spit on her pussy, then run my finger through it, spreading the wetness through her center, pushing it inside her, pumping once, twice.

I hear her suck in a breath, and she grabs my head with both of her hands.

"Casey," she pants.

"You want my mouth or my fingers?" I circle her clit with the tip of my tongue.

"Both," she stutters.

I add another finger and push inside her while sucking on her clit. I don't want to make her come yet though, so I keep my pace slow, despite the way she's starting to pull on my hair and hold me in place. It turns me on, but I really don't want to blow, so I'll set the pace. I want us both coming together tonight.

When I've reached my own limit, I pull back and remove my fingers.

"Wait, what are you doing?" She looks down at me, confused and a whole lot turned on.

"I'm getting into the shower." I stand and take her by the waist and lift her off the counter. "Gotta get this paint off, and the water's gonna get cold." I kiss her lips softly.

She shakes her head, frustrated, but she lets me take her hand and lead her into the shower.

I stand directly under the spray and release her hands to rub the paint that she smeared on my face off. She places her hands on my hips while I do, and she slowly drifts her hands around to my ass, pulling me in closer to her. I wipe the water from my face and look at her.

Her gaze is intense, her hands on my body confident. "Casey, I want you so bad that I can't see straight. I need you tonight. No more waiting."

Instead of answering her, I lift her in my arms, and she wraps her legs around my waist. My dick is like steel, resting against her pussy.

"You want me right here? Right now?" I kiss her, tongue sliding inside her mouth.

She tilts her head to take the kiss deeper, making me groan when she sucks on my tongue.

I rock my hips just enough so my cock glides through her center, hitting her clit. She sucks harder on my tongue with every slide. And when my head reaches her opening, she stops sucking and pulls back to look at me. I push in, just enough to feel her heat cover my crown, making us both moan.

"Fuck."

"Deeper," she says.

So, I push in a little more and then more, but not to the hilt. I really don't want to fuck her for the first time in the shower, but damn does she feel good. I pull my hips back and out of her completely, then set her down.

"What are you doing?" She runs her hands up my chest. "I thought I was pretty clear, but maybe not." Her hands move back down my chest, over my abdomen, and then she takes hold of my cock.

"Oh, no. You're pretty fucking clear. I just want to be able to see you in every way, so we're going to get this paint off and get to the bedroom as fast as we can."

I turn us so she's under the spray, and she lets go of me. Then I reach over and get some shampoo and massage it into her hair. Her eyes don't leave mine.

After I rinse her hair, then take care of mine at lightning speed, I step out and grab a towel for her and wrap it around her body. Then I grab my towel and tie it around my waist, take her hand and hightail it across the hall to my room. As soon as we're inside, I lock the door and loosen the knot at my waist, letting my towel drop to the floor. She releases hers, and it pools at her feet. I have to bite my lip to keep from groaning at the sight of her.

Her skin glistens, still damp from the shower. Droplets fall from her hair, trailing over her full breasts, down her soft, flat stomach, and along the curve of her hips that drive me insane before disappearing over the length of her perfectly toned legs. If it didn't mean I'd have to fight off every man on the planet, I'd tell her she should walk around naked all the time. She's far too fine to cover up.

I move toward her, stopping just in front of her so we're close, but our bodies are not touching, which is near impossible with my dick rock hard, and run my hands into her hair.

"You sure about this?" I ask her, just so there is no misunderstanding what's gonna happen here.

"Oh, I'm so sure. I need you inside me. No more waiting."

She backs us up to the bed, and I drop my hands from her head. When she sits on the bed, she scoots backward to lie on the pillows.

Before I follow, I turn and grab some condoms out of my top dresser drawer and toss them on the bed next to her.

She looks down and sees the strip. "You think we need all those?"

"We're not leaving this bed tonight. I've waited for far too long for this, and I'm making every fucking second count." I start trailing kisses up her leg, and when I reach her center, I put her leg over my shoulder and run my tongue from her core to her clit.

"Casey … oh … that feels so good." Her hands tug at my hair.

I swirl my tongue a few more times, then continue kissing her—making a meal of this moment as I make my way up her stomach, paying homage to her naval, lavishing her breasts and the sweet nipples I love so much, and up her neck that's become like home to me. I caress her jaw until I reach her lips, my body on top of hers, perfectly aligned with hers, as it should be.

Her legs open, and I sink my hips between her thighs.

She lets out a soft moan when my shaft rubs against her clit as I slide it to her center, her wetness coating me. "Fuck."

Her arms wrap around my waist, and I take her ass in my hands. When she rocks her hips, my dick pushes inside of her, and we both stop moving.

"Let me put on a condom."

I start to lift off of her, but she stops me.

"You know I've been on the pill for a while now, and after Trey, I got tested, and I'm clean. I want to feel you. All of you."

I nod because words aren't coming.

"Yeah?" she questions, looking a little nervous.

"Yes. Fuck yes. I was tested before camp, and I'm clean." I lean down and kiss her. This kiss is wet and dirty.

I pull my hips back and line up with her pussy, then slowly push in. She breaks our kiss, moaning as I hit as deep as I can.

"Oh fuck, you feel good. There's no way I'll be able to make this last."

She starts to grind against me, circling her hips. "Please, Casey."

Who am I to deny her? This girl owns every part of me.

I push up onto my hands to look at her. "I got you, pretty girl." And I do.

One hand still braces my upper body, but I wrap my other hand around her thigh and push so her knee is bent. The new angle of her hips makes me reach deeper inside of her.

We rock together, and our pace quickens with every thrust. I can feel her walls start to tighten around me, so I know she's getting close to coming.

"Come, pretty girl. Soak my cock. Let me feel you fall apart. For me. Only for me."

"Casey," she breathes. "I'm gonna come. Oh God, I'm so close."

Our bodies start to lose rhythm as we both get closer to orgasm. I release her leg, and she wraps it around my waist. I drop down to my elbows, bracing her face.

"You're so beautiful." I thrust into her deeply. "You were made for me."

I bend my head and take her mouth, our tongues twirling. But when I feel her orgasm hit, I pull back so I can watch her come. Our eyes lock, and as I feel her walls contract around my cock, I start to come.

This isn't just sex. This is complete connection. And I'm never letting her go.

The words I've wanted to say for so long are tumbling out of my mouth before I can stop them. "I love you, Noelle. You are my everything."

A tear runs out of the corner of her eye, but she smiles. "I love you, Casey."

As we both come down from our orgasms, I pull out and lie beside her. I bring her into me, and she rests her head on my chest and drapes her leg over mine.

I can feel her breathing change as she drifts off to sleep. I can't help but think that this might possibly be the best day of my life. But it's not just because of the sex. It's more than that. It's always been more with Noelle.

If, tomorrow, she says this isn't real, I might never recover.

TWENTY

NOELLE

CHELSEA and I both have a free day today, so we decide to go get coffees and mani and pedis. It's packed in the salon, but we manage to get seats next to each other on the side that is separated from the other seats.

"What color are you getting?" I hold out the color samples to her.

"I'm thinking I'll go bold. Like a nice bright orange or something. Really live it up." She laughs.

"Hmm, I like that idea. Maybe I'll do a deep red though. I feel like that's not only fall vibes, but also Walker colors. I need my toes to match my jersey." I hand her the samples, then take a drink of my pumpkin spice latte.

"No one will see your toes at the game though. It's too cold to wear flip-flops." She flips through the colors. "Unless you want Casey to notice. Please tell me he doesn't have some kind of foot fetish."

"Eww, no! That's so gross, Chels!" I smack her arm lightly, making her laugh. "I just thought it would be cute. Go Stallions!" I hold my hands out and wiggle them, smiling.

"I mean, you never know. It's always the sweet, hot guys that surprise you." She gives me a wink.

"Well, I assure you, Casey doesn't have a foot fetish. Oh, but maybe I should get his number on my thumbs. That would be cute, right?" I smile and raise my brows.

"This is the one!" She hands the color to the technician. It's not quite neon, but definitely a bold orange. "Okay, sorry. Back to you. Casey's number, thumbs." She nods. "Yeah, that would be cute."

"Yay! I can't wait to show him. He'll love that." I pull out my phone, snap a selfie, and send it to him. I haven't seen him yet today or really talked to him much since he had practice and film after.

"So, can I ask you something without coming across too nosy?" She looks at me pointedly.

"Yeah, of course." I smile at her.

"Are you guys, like, officially dating now, or are you still tiptoeing around your feelings, or what?" She smirks.

"What do you mean, tiptoeing around our feelings?" I laugh nervously because this is actually something I've been thinking about since we had sex.

"I mean, it's none of my business, but I was just curious. When we were at their house, watching the out-of-town game, and his sister brought up that you guys were together, I was happy to hear it. Y'all are cute together." She smiles, then takes a sip of her matcha.

"Honestly, I'm not sure. I mean ..." I pause. "Can I tell you something?" I ask.

"Yes, of course." She nods.

"Well, you know what happened with me and Trey?" I ask her.

"I do. I never liked him, for the record." She points at me.

"Yeah, he's not a great guy." I breathe in. "So, I ran into him on campus one day, and he figured out my schedule and started following me."

"Jesus, Noelle. Why didn't you tell me?" she says, concerned.

I lean in closer to her. "Well, I was just trying to ignore him, but one day, he grabbed me and was spouting off how I was his, and I just blurted out that I was dating Casey." I shake my head. "So, then I had to tell Casey to go along with it, just in case it got around somehow." I look down at my hands twisting together on my lap. "Basically, it started as fake, but I'm not so sure that it is anymore. At least not for me. But I don't know if I should say anything because what if he doesn't feel the same way?"

Chelsea's head drops back, and she barks out a laugh.

"Why are you laughing? This is a slight crisis for me. He's my best friend, and I'm falling in love with him, but I'm not sure what to do about it." I sigh.

"I'm sorry. I promise I'm not laughing at you." She reaches over and takes my hand. "I'm just laughing because that boy is head over heels in love with you. Honestly, I thought you knew it and were just keeping him in the friend zone because you didn't feel the same."

"Are you serious? Why do you think that?" Now I really want to know what she sees that I'm not.

"Well, for starters, he was always around the dorms our freshman year, and you guys spent a lot of time together, even after you and Trey started dating." She pauses to take a drink. "I didn't get to see you as much last year, but I'm betting you spent about the same amount of time with him?"

I nod.

"And now that we live together, I see it. From him helping us move in to the little things he does for you. Like, he checks to see if you need anything before he comes over, and he pays attention to details, like when you're getting low on toothpaste. But mostly, it's in the way he looks at you. That boy looks at you like he's been in love with you forever and he's just waiting for you to figure it out." She smiles softly. "I had to learn at an early age how to read people. Emotions specifically. And I'm telling you, he loves you."

There's a lump in my throat, and I feel like I can't speak. I want to believe that everything she's saying is true. That it's real. Because I do love Casey.

"Are you guys acting with all things, or have you slept together? Like, what's part of the deal?" She props her hand on her chin and leans in closer.

"Well … here's the other embarrassing piece of all of this." I cover my face with my hands. "I asked him to teach me how to be better in bed."

She doesn't say anything, so I uncover my eyes and look over at her.

"You're not a virgin though, right?" she questions.

"No, but Trey was my first, and according to him, I didn't know what I was doing in the bedroom, so I don't know … I guess I wanted to see what I was doing wrong, and Casey seemed to be the best person to ask." I shrug. "It sounds so stupid when I say all of this out loud, but it really messed with my head. And when I walked in on him and Zoey that day, they were going at it in a way we never did. Like, completely different. When we were together, it was all very vanilla, I guess you would say." I shake my head. "Like, he never wanted to do anything that made me feel good. My first orgasm was with Casey, and Trey and I were together off and on for nearly two years."

"Honestly, that doesn't surprise me in the least. You know he's a narcissist, right? I wasn't even around much to see you together, but I could spot it from a mile away." She places her hand back on top of mine. "Look, everything that Trey might have said or done means nothing. It's going to take some time, but he actually did you a favor. Because you might not have seen his true colors until even more damage was done."

"See, like, logically, I know this, but I just don't understand how I could have been so wrong about someone. I know he was my first boyfriend, but seriously, Chelsea, how could I have been so stupid?" I lean my head back on the seat and close my eyes to keep the tears from falling.

"Noelle, you cannot blame yourself. He was a master manipulator, and sadly, he knew all the right things to say and do to ultimately make you doubt yourself. About everything. Am I right?" She squeezes my hand.

I look at her. "Yeah, it was definitely a gradual process, looking back. He would say things about my friends and how he didn't like certain people—"

She interrupts, "Let me guess. I was one of those people?"

I feel awkward answering, so I just nod, my face scrunching. "I'm sorry. It wasn't just you though. He really hated Casey, as you can imagine. Trey just couldn't understand how and why we were so close. A few months after we started dating, we got into a big fight because he thought Casey was trying to break us up."

"Was he?" She smirks.

"No. I mean, I knew Casey didn't like Trey, but he never did anything to try to break us up." I let go of her hand and take a drink of my coffee.

"Listen, he never deserved you. Casey absolutely does. He's one of the good ones for sure. And you don't have to give me details, but is he as good in bed as I think he would be?" She wiggles her brows.

I can't help but laugh. "My experience is limited, but, yeah … it's been amazing. Mostly because he's let me try things and not be embarrassed about it. But I think the best thing is how generous he is, if you know what I mean." I can feel my face flush.

"I'm not sure that I do. Tell me more." She cracks up, which also makes me laugh. "I'm kidding, but also not. Tell me all the things you feel comfortable sharing."

"Well, up until a few nights ago, we had just been doing oral." Again, my face feels like it's on fire with embarrassment that I'm saying any of this out loud in front of the nail technicians. "But we finally had sex the other night, and I swear I felt like I left my body." We both laugh. "With everything we had done leading up to that being incredible, I didn't doubt that it would be good, and I was getting pretty impatient, but, good Lord, he knows what to do."

"I'm so happy for you, truly. You're, like, having your sexual awakening! It's so exciting!" She claps her hands, and people look at us. "Sorry!" She grimaces.

"Okay, but seriously, what should I do? We said I love you, but we also always say that—like, not daily—so how do I know if it's an *I love ya, pal* or an *I love you madly and deeply*?"

"Did you say it during or after sex?"

"Yes, we both said it right after, but then when I left the next day, nothing. But I think maybe he wanted to?" I shrug.

"So, I think when it comes to Casey, you can't let any of the physical get in the way of how you normally communicate. You tell him everything, so don't be afraid to talk to him about this. I understand how you feel about not trusting yourself, but Casey is a constant for you and has never hurt you or made you feel bad about yourself. He's your number one cheerleader. Trust that and be honest with him about your feelings. Just tell him. Tell him you don't want this to be fake anymore. I guarantee you it will work out. And probably lead to some insanely good orgasms." She laughs.

"You're right. I need to trust my gut and just talk to him. I'm just scared it will ruin our friendship if it doesn't work out or if he doesn't feel the same." My phone chimes with a text from Casey.

> Casey: Hey, pretty girl. Getting manis and pedis without me?

Yes, Casey has come with me on occasion. He loves pedicures, and I absolutely love that he does.

> Noelle: Sorry! Chelsea and I both had a day off, so we got coffee and then came here.

"Is that him?" she asks.

"Yeah, it is." I'm sure I have a dopey smile on my face.

> Casey: Text me when you're done or just come over. Or I can come to yours, if you want. Either way, I really want to see you. I've missed you today.

I heart the message, then tell him I'll text him when we're done. I know Chelsea is right. I just need to bite the bullet and spill it all. And then I need to trust that everything will be okay. That I won't lose my best friend.

TWENTY-ONE

CASEY

THIS WEEK IS a big game against our rival, Chandler State. We beat them last year and hope to keep the Golden Hat for another year. It's a trophy that's been passed between the two universities for decades. It's tradition, and it also comes with bragging rights. The game is off campus between the two schools, but closer to Walker this year.

They're having a good season, just like we are, but they'll be out for revenge, so it's likely going to be a brutal game. The music is thumping in the locker room, everyone even more pumped up than usual. In games like this, you have to be hungry to win. If you aren't, your opponent will do everything they can to distract you, wear you down, and run you into the ground.

A few of the guys on D-line are getting into teammates' faces.

"You want this? You gotta earn it, son. You gonna win today? You gotta fight for it. You gonna fight today, Smith? You hungry?" Sam Holland, one of our linemen, yells in Smith's face.

"Fuck yeah!" Smith shouts.

Coach walks in then, followed by Archie fuckin' Griffith. His hair is a little shorter, and he's wearing jeans, a Walker football polo and hat, cowboy boots, and a big-ass belt buckle.

I look over at Beck. "Did you know he was coming today?"

Beck has a smirk on his face. "I had no idea, but I'm not at all surprised. They have a Monday night game this week. Haven't talked to him for a few weeks. Just a couple of texts here and there."

Archie walks around the room, smacking helmets, bumping fists, slapping hands. When he gets to Beck and me, he grabs us both in a hug.

"You fuckers didn't think I'd miss this, did you?" He chuckles.

"Glad you're here, man! The girls come with you?"

He got engaged in the spring and has a new baby—or I guess, not brand-new. I don't know baby stuff.

"Yeah, Emma's parents are moving down this week, and we're helping wrap up a few things. We'll come by the house tomorrow, and we'll chat some more. Emma has the baby on the sideline, waiting for me to come back out, but I had to drop in and see my boys!" We do a handshake, and then he turns to Beck to do the same. "You ready, Linson?"

Beck nods. "You know it. Always ready."

Coach comes to stand in the center of the room. "All right, boys, bring it in."

We all move in closer, forming a circle around Coach Pettys.

"We have a job to do today. And you've worked hard. We have an opportunity, and we're gonna take it. You gotta believe in yourself and your team. You gotta believe it in here." He points to his heart. "Every whistle, every down, every play is the play we put them on their backs. Every play is the play we get the touchdown. Work together, communicate, find your balance, find your center of gravity and stay in it. We're gonna bring the house down, boys. And we're gonna keep that motherfuckin' hat at home! Stallions on three. One! Two! Three!"

We all have our hands up, with our index fingers pointing up, and shout together, "STALLIONS!"

It's these moments I love about the game. The brotherhood, the bond we make as a team … there's nothing like it.

"As you see, we have a guest today. Griff, you gonna take us out?" Coach points at Archie, standing next to me and Beck.

"Hell fuckin' yeah, Coach!" Archie claps his hands together and starts pacing the room in a circle. "Stallions, are you ready?! You ready to turn up on these boys." Clap. "Smash these boys?"

A collective, "Hell yeah," rings out.

"We will hit all day."

"Yes, sir."

"We are motivated."

"Yes, sir."

"We are dedicated."

"Yes, sir."

"We are the best on the field."

"Yes, sir."

Archie stops walking and stands in the center of the room. He looks around, nodding. "We gonna take it all day like—"

We clap.

"To the blue." Clap.

"To the white." Clap.

"To the offense like—" Clap.

"To the defense like—" Clap.

"To the house like—" Clap.

"And it sounds like—"

We all start jumping around, chanting, getting pumped up.

"And it sounds like—"

We chant louder.

"And it sounds like—"

"WIN!" we yell.

"Let's go protect what belongs to us!" he yells.

We grab our helmets and run out of the locker room and

through the tunnel and wait. The adrenaline is high, and we're ready to bust out onto the field. And we do just that when we hear our band play our fight song.

Beck and I usually stay together from the locker room, to the tunnel, to running out, to setting our gear next to each other. We've played together since we were kids, and some things you just don't change. I get to play a game I love with my best friend. Doesn't get any better than this.

We get to the bench and both look into the stands for our families. His dad and sister are sitting next to my parents, Charlie, Noelle, Arbor, and Chelsea. They're all waving at us.

Then my sister pulls out a poster board that says, *The weather may be cool, but #24 is hot.* Then she turns it around, and it says, *President of the Beckham Linson Fan Club #24.*

I look over at Beck and see the smile he reserves for my sister. He loves it, but he loves it because he knows it makes her happy and she likely thinks she's the funniest person ever.

When I turn back to wave to Noelle one more time, she has a sign too. Hers says, *#82 is my boyfriend* with hearts all over it. I bring my palm to my heart, then blow her a kiss.

If she means to make a statement, she did. And I'm not gonna let her take it back.

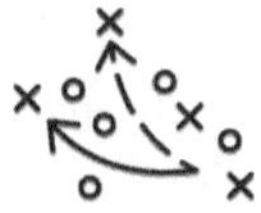

This might just be my best game of the season. We're up by twenty points, and two of those touchdowns ... are mine. And I want one more to end the game.

We have the ball on the four-yard line, so the plan is to pass off to Beck for him to plow through and run it in. But the defense blitzes, and Bo is under pressure in the pocket. I get around the cornerback guarding me and run diagonally to get to a position where Bo can pass me the ball.

When he throws the ball, the cornerback is at my front, holding on to my right arm, trying to block the pas—or worse, intercept it. I jump up and reach for the ball in the air, grabbing it with my left hand. One-handed.

My teammates run to me, jumping up and down, cheering, yelling, smacking my helmet and shoulder pads. I can hear the crowd going wild, which just amps me up even more. I'm not known to be a showboater, but I can't help it. After tossing the ball to the referee, I turn and face the crowd, arms up, waving my hands toward me. The crowd gets louder, and then I take a bow, turn, and run back to the sideline.

As I pass Coach, he grabs my face mask to stop me. "You are feelin' it today, King! That's what I'm talkin' about!" He releases the face mask and smacks the top of my helmet.

I take it off as I walk away and look up to my family. They're all clapping, and the girls are jumping up and down. When I make eye contact with Noelle, I hold up four fingers and then point to her. The smile she gives me is better than any touchdown I scored today.

Four minutes later, the game ends, and the fans rush the field. They're not supposed to, but with this rivalry, the university is willing to pay the fines. I push my way through the crowd to where the team is gathering for the Golden Hat presentation and look around to see if Noelle and my family have made it on to the field, but I don't see them yet.

Just as we're finishing up the team pictures, I spot them near the tunnel we'll take to get to the locker room. I run up to Noelle, drop my helmet on the ground, and lift her in my arms.

"You were amazing!" She laughs as I spin her around.

"You like that one-hander? That was pretty epic." I laugh.

When I set her on the ground, I take her face in my hands and kiss her.

"Good game, King!" people shout as they walk by me.

Noelle pulls away, and her cheeks are pink. "That catch was electric!"

"Little brother! You killed it out there today!" My sister bounces over, and I give her a side hug.

"Thank you, thank you."

She's older than me by, like, two minutes, but whatever. I'll let her have it this time.

I feel a pull on the back of my shoulder pad, making me turn. It's Archie, Emma, and their baby, Lainey, who is wearing little pink headphones over her wild curls.

"Dude, you were fire today! What a game!"

"Congrats, Casey!" Emma leans in for a hug.

"Thanks, guys. It was a good time for sure." I lean toward Lainey, who is in Archie's arms. "Hi, Lainey! Go Stallions!" I hold up my index finger, and she grabs it in her hand and gives me a drooly smile.

I look at Archie, and we laugh. It's wild to see one of my best friends with a baby already. But he's a natural, and I love seeing them happy.

"You guys hanging around, or do you need to get back to Dallas in the morning?"

"We'll have to leave tomorrow afternoon, but I'm hoping to hang out with my boys before we head out."

We do a handshake.

"Yeah, for sure." I turn to my side and reach for Noelle's hand.

"Ahh-haaa. Okay … so you finally grew some balls and went for it. Good for you, buddy!" Archie slaps me on the shoulder. "How you doin', Noelle? It's good to see you." He leans over and hugs her.

"Hey, Archie. Hey, Emma. Good to see you guys too." She smiles at them both. "Hi, Lainey." She waves at the baby. "She's beautiful. Did she do okay here at the game?"

"Oh, yeah, she's used to having the noise-canceling headphones on at Archie's games." Emma smooths a hand over Lainey's back.

"My little sunshine is a perfect angel, aren't you?" He leans in and kisses her head. "We should head out though. It'll be late by the time we get back to Emma's parents', and we need to get her to bed. I'll text you in the morning, and we'll work something out, yeah?" He holds out his fist for a bump.

"Sounds good, man. Good to see you guys." I give Emma another hug and pat Lainey's back.

"Darlin', let's say goodbye to Linson and Charlie, and then we'll go." He wraps an arm around Emma's waist, and they head to my sister and Beck.

I take Noelle's hand and pull her into me again. "Hey, so I loved your sign. Was that your idea or my sister's?" I don't wait for an answer and kiss her.

She pulls back from the kiss. "Well, Charlie was making one and happened to have another poster, so I thought it would be fun." She shrugs.

"I loved it." I tilt her chin up with my thumb and finger. "And I love you." I can't even hold it in.

Neither one of us has said it since the night we had sex, but I'm tired of staying quiet.

A smile breaks across her face. "I love you too."

I feel like a million fucking dollars right now. "You coming over tonight?"

"I planned on it. But if you're too tired, I can go to my place." She lifts a shoulder.

"Fuck no. I want you at my place. Did you ride with my sister?" I tuck a piece of hair behind her ear.

She nods. "Yeah, I did."

"Okay, pretty girl. I'll see you later." I give her one last kiss, say goodbye to my parents and my sister, and nudge Beck's shoulder with mine. "Let's roll, brother."

We walk into the tunnel toward the locker room, recapping the game, and I can't wait to celebrate with my team, but I also can't wait to get home to my girl.

CHAPTER
TWENTY-TWO

CASEY

NOELLE and I spent all night celebrating the win. Naked. This girl blows my mind in every way. I said it before, and I'll say it again: Trey was a fucking idiot. She knows exactly how to use her body, and she drives me fucking wild. I will say, she's gotten much more confident, and she isn't afraid to ask for what she wants. And watching her discover what feels good for her is a privilege.

We're meeting up with Archie and Emma before they head back to Dallas today. Noelle ran home to change and told me she would meet me there. So, my sister, Beck, Bo, and Silas grab a ride with me to Logan's. It was Archie's pick because he misses their wings or something.

The first thing I see when we walk in is Trey. He's sitting with some other guys on the baseball team, who are actually decent guys. I'm not sure why they hang around Trey. We make eye contact as I pass, and he fucking smirks at me.

Beck must see it because he grabs my shoulder and squeezes it. "Keep moving, man."

"Fucking hate him so much." I shake my head.

"Yeah, me too, but you got the girl, so let's chill with our friends and get some food. I'm starving." Beck smacks my back as we approach our table.

"There you are! What took you guys so long? We've been here for, like, thirty minutes." Archie holds up both of his hands.

"No, we have not. Don't listen to him. He's just hungry." Emma laughs and rolls her eyes.

"Hey, guys!" My sister hugs Emma first, then hugs Archie.

"What up, Chuck?! Good to see you. You keeping Linson in line?" He winks at her and then looks at Beck. He loves to rile him up.

"You know it." She holds out her hands to Emma, who's holding Lainey. "Can I hold her?"

"Of course! She just ate, so be careful about bouncing her around too much. She might spit up on you." She hands Charlie the baby.

"That's okay. She's too pretty to get upset about a little spit-up." Charlie cradles Lainey in her arms and kisses her forehead.

"My little sunshine can do no wrong. Even poopy diapers are cute with her." Archie puts his arm around Emma.

"Great. Then you can handle all of them!" She smacks his chest.

We all laugh. Then the girls start talking about baby things and what's new.

"Callaway, it's good to see you, man. You're having a great season. How you feelin'?" Archie asks him.

"Thanks. I appreciate it. I feel pretty good. One more year, I think, and then I'll make some decisions on declaring for the draft." Bo nods and taps the table.

"Yeah, I think one more season would do you some good. Skill-wise, you're ready, but pro-level ball is a different ball game, you know." Archie sits up and leans on the table.

"That's what I was thinking. I'd like to bulk up a little more too." Bo sits back in his chair and crosses his arms.

"Arbuckle? How you liking Walker? Big change from Georgia?" Archie asks him.

"I love it. Program is definitely run differently, but that's why I'm here." He twists the hat on his head backward.

"You're in the best place you can be. What about you, Linson? You're declaring this year, right?" Archie tips his head at Beck.

"That's the plan. I wanna finish this season strong, then start preparing for the combine right away, like you did. I don't want to take a break at all." Beck's arm is around my sister's shoulders as he talks. If they're in the same room, he has to be touching her. And I get it now. I can't keep my hands off Noelle when she's around.

"Yeah, you have to jump right in to keep your motivation going. But also stay in peak shape." Archie nods, then looks at me. "How about you, King? You staying one more season, right?"

"One more year for me, yeah. Since I didn't play much my freshman year, I want to get one more full season in." I nod, then look toward the door, anxious for Noelle to get here.

"Lookin' for someone?" Archie smirks.

"Yep, waiting for Noelle. Her ex is here, so I want to try to get to her before she sees that he's here." I lift my chin in the direction that Trey is sitting in.

"I'm proud of you, King. Finally got your girl. How did that happen?" He smiles and nods.

"Well, it's complicated, but let's go with, the timing was right." I shrug.

"Timing is everything. Right, Em?" He puts his arm back around Emma.

"What's that?" She turns from my sister and looks at him.

"Timing. If you hadn't gone to that party at Smith's that night and I hadn't knocked you up, we might not have been together. But there was a bigger plan. Right, baby?" He leans over and kisses her.

"Exactly, and I wouldn't change a thing." She kisses him this time.

I look over at the door again. It opens, and my girl is standing there, light shining behind her, making her look like a goddamn goddess. She sees me and waves and starts walking toward me, but Trey has the fucking nerve to walk up to her and grab her elbow. I'm on my feet before I can think, my chair falling to the floor, and I'm across the restaurant before the motherfucker has a chance to blink.

"Get your fucking hands off her." I insert myself between them, knocking his hand from her elbow and creating a wall between them.

"Just talking to her, King." He smirks. "Isn't that right, Noelle?"

I don't look behind me to see Noelle's face, but she grabs my biceps and squeezes. "Casey, don't. Come on. Let's just go. It's fine."

"There a problem over here?" Beck asks, Archie and Bo standing behind him.

Trey's friends then stand and get behind him.

"Nah, no problem. Just trying to understand why Noelle didn't reply to my text the other day." He fucking smiles and looks directly at me.

I look over my shoulder.

Noelle's eyes are wide, and she's shaking her head. "Trey, stop it." She tugs on my arm and comes to my side. "Come on. Let's just go."

"You go ahead. Charlie and Emma are over there with the baby. I'll be there in a second. I just want to have a chat with Trey." I kiss her on the forehead, then look at Trey, whose jaw is clenched.

"Casey, please. It's not worth it."

My sister walks up then and takes Noelle's hand. "Come sit with me. It'll be fine."

She pulls Noelle away, whose eyes are pleading, but I give her a small smile and nod.

"It's okay, Noelle. You can sit and watch. This guy is all talk and no action. You'll see," Trey calls after her.

"Don't fucking look at her or talk to her. You don't even deserve to breathe the same air." I seethe.

"See, King, I would leave her alone, but she keeps replying to my texts." He smiles and holds his hands up. "So, that tells me she's not really over me. And just in case you need the reminder … she's mine. She's been mine since freshman year. She's been mine since you and Linson came over and threatened me to stay away from her freshman year. And she's been mine since she made me a promise to come with me when I get drafted this year." He leans closer, his voice lower, as if he's gonna tell me a secret. "You know how I know that? Because I claimed that pussy, and therefore, it will always be mine. Every time you put your cum in there, know I already smothered it with my own. I. Own. It."

Before I can think about what I'm doing, my fist flies, and I knock him back into his friends, who hold him up. Blood gushes from his nose, down his mouth, but he still smiles.

Noelle comes running back to us, but Beck grabs her by the waist to keep her away.

"Casey, please stop!" she cries out.

"That all you got, pussy?" Trey taunts as he wipes his nose with the back of his hand. "Or do you need your buddies to step in and help?"

I lift my arm to hit him again, but Archie steps between us.

"I think it's best you leave, don't you?" He pushes a finger into Trey's chest.

"Fuck you, Griffith. Why are you here anyway? And you brought your baby into a fucking bar? Go back to Dallas." Trey spits blood and nearly hits Archie's boot.

Archie just laughs. "You a fan, Trey? You know where I live? That's cute." He tips his chin toward his friends. "Now, boys, we don't need to make this worse, do we? I hate to break that pitching arm of yours, Trey." He leans in. "My fiancée might get real mad at me if I have to beat your ass in this bar. And I still haven't had my wings yet, and that's the only reason we came to Logan's today."

One of the guys steps up and puts a hand on Trey's shoulder. "We got it, Griff. There's no problem here." He pulls on Trey's shoulder. "Let's go, man. We ain't stepping in to save your ass." The guy tips his chin at us. "Great game yesterday, boys. Sorry about him."

Trey jerks out of his hold and stalks to the door, pushing it so hard that it hits the wall outside.

"What a baby," Beck chirps.

The baseball players follow Trey out, and then Archie wraps an arm around me and pulls me in the direction of our table. I look down at my hand and see blood on my knuckles.

"I'll be right back." I walk past the table, not looking at the girls.

Beck follows me into the restroom. "You got one in, Case. Now let it go. She's yours, and you know it."

I shake my head back and forth as I rinse the blood off my hand. "He's fucking vile. What he said about Noelle ..." I seethe, just thinking about the prick. "He's been texting her, and she didn't tell me."

"I'm sure she had her reasons. Try not to read into it too much."

I look up, and we make eye contact in the mirror.

"Talk to her."

I nod. "I just don't understand why she wouldn't tell me."

"Case, she's with you. That's all you need to know. The rest, it's just noise." He tips his head toward the door. "Now let's go eat some wings with our friends, and then you can talk to her when we get home."

"I'll be there in a minute." I grab a paper towel and dry my hands.

He doesn't say anything in response and walks out.

I know he's right, but Trey has fucked with her for far too long. For two years, I watched as she ran back to him, mistake after mistake. He said he owns her. He did, for a long time. Not just her body, but her mind. Is it possible he still has a hold on her?

I stand and run my fingers through my hair and take a deep breath to calm myself down. Outside of football, I've never hit anyone, and I don't regret it now. Even when Beck and I paid him a visit last year, before he even cheated, I didn't hit him then, even though I really, really wanted to. But I'm not that guy. That's not the man I want to be for her. And what if she is texting him back? She's taken him back before. Who's to say she wouldn't again? I like to think we're enough, that we're more than what they had, but he planted that doubt, and now I need to know.

When I get back to the table, there are baskets of wings and French fries sitting in the center of the table. Thankfully, no one says anything to me, and they act as if nothing happened. I don't want to talk about it in front of everyone. Besides, Archie is leaving soon, and we don't get much time with him now.

Noelle places her hand on my leg, eyes full of worry. "You okay?"

I place my hand on top of hers. "I'm fine." I give her a strained smile.

We join in on the group conversation as we eat, but I notice Noelle hasn't eaten much, so I know she's upset too. Yeah, we're gonna need to talk this out. No more guessing where I stand with her, whether this is real or still just a ruse. I'm gonna lay it all out. Tell her that I want her. My heart belongs to her. Always has, always will.

TWENTY-THREE

NOELLE

TODAY DID NOT TURN out like I'd thought it would. After an amazing night with Casey, I was looking forward to hanging out with his friends because, well, they're fun, but also, I know he misses having Archie around.

We finished up our lunch, and we're outside the restaurant now, saying our goodbyes. Emma hugs us all, then gets Lainey in her car seat as Archie hugs everyone.

"We'll see you all soon. Maybe after Christmas or something, yeah?" He starts to walk around the front of his truck. "Be safe on and off the field." He winks and waves as he gets in the driver's side.

We stand there and wave as they honk, then drive off.

"Okay, that was fun. How freakin' cute is that baby?! I could eat her up." Charlie grabs Beck's arm.

He smiles and shakes his head. "She's really cute."

"Char, no. No babies yet. I'm not ready to be an uncle," Casey teases.

"Settle down, Case. We have lots to do before we have babies. Right, Beck?" She stands on her tiptoes and kisses his cheek.

He wraps his arm around her waist and lifts her up to kiss her lips. "Yes, like going home and taking a nap."

Casey takes his keys out of his pocket and tosses them to Beck. "You guys take my truck home. I'll ride with Noelle."

Charlie comes over to me and hugs me. "Talk to him, okay?" she whispers in my ear.

I nod, and when she pulls back, I smile. "I will."

Bo and Silas come over to me next and give me a hug. Since I spend so much time at the house, I've gotten to know Bo and Silas better, and I'd definitely consider them friends now. They're both total sweethearts, and Bo is seriously driven to succeed.

"See ya." He rubs my head, messing up my hair, making pieces fall out of my ponytail.

"Hey!" I laugh and fix my hair.

Casey takes my hand in his and waves to everyone. "Later."

"I had to park in the back." I steer him toward the alley that leads to the parking lot in the back of the restaurant.

"You want me to drive?" he asks.

"It doesn't matter to me. If you want to, you can." Even though I have a push-start, I hand him my keys to unlock the doors.

He walks me to the passenger side and opens it for me. Once I'm in, he closes the door and walks around the back to the driver's side.

I watch him as he gets into the car. I have an SUV, but he still looks like he has to fold his legs into the car—they're so long. He adjusts the seat, then turns to look at me.

"We should talk," he says.

I know we should. For many reasons, but it stirs my nerves that he's the one to bring it up. I was kind of hoping to ease into the conversation. He seemed to be less tense by the time we finished lunch, but I guess not.

"Okay," I say quietly. "Yeah, we should."

He starts to drive, and we're quiet for the five minutes it takes us to get from Campus Corner to Duck Pond Park. When he pulls into the parking lot, there are a few cars scattered, but it's chilly today, so not many people are outside from what I can tell.

He puts the car in park and turns to face me. "First thing I want to say is that I'm sorry you had to see that today, but I'm not sorry I hit him. He deserved it and then some. But what I want to know is how long he's been texting you, and are you still talking to him?"

"God, no! I mean, yes, he has been texting me, but I don't talk to him. I block him every time he texts me from a new number." I reach for his hand, but he pulls it away.

"How long?" he asks.

"Well, you know he was texting me this summer, but I blocked him on his main number and on Instagram." I shake my head. "Then when we got to school and after I ran into him, he texted me from an unknown number, and I blocked him again."

"Is that it?" He raises his brows questioningly.

"It's probably been about a month since I last heard from him. So, I've handled it. It's fine, Casey, really." I lay my head back on the headrest.

"No, Noelle. It's not fine. He's harassing you, even if you aren't responding. My job is to protect you, and I can't do that if you keep secrets from me." He raises his voice, frustrated.

"I'm not keeping secrets from you! I didn't want to make it into a big deal because it's not!" I shout.

"But you did! You kept it from me. What would have happened if it had gotten worse, and I didn't know?" he yells.

"I didn't tell you because I was handling it! I was taking care of it on my own! You're always there for me, I know. But I don't want Trey in our space anymore!" I reach for him, and he pulls away again.

"You don't have to take care of it on your own though! I love you. I'm in love with you. And if I get my wish, I get to keep you forever. Don't you understand that?" He holds his hands out in front of him.

"Well, I love you too! And I want you to keep me forever because I'm keeping you too!" Tears start running down my face, and I can't control it.

Casey and I never fight. Never even disagree much, so the fact that we're yelling at each other is just … wrong.

"Hey, don't cry." His voice softens. "I'm sorry. I just got so pissed off when he was taunting me, and then I got upset that you didn't tell me." He puts his hand on my face and wipes my tears with his thumb.

"And I understand that. I really do. He's literally the worst. In all ways." I sniff. "But I also feel like he did me a favor."

"What do you mean?" He tilts his head.

"Well, for starters, he cheated on me and got caught made me realize that I was done for good. And I have no doubt that it wasn't the first time he'd cheated. Then he was following me around like a creeper at the beginning of school. But that day, when I told him I was dating you, it was such a natural response. And even though it might have started out as a lie, I think it was maybe divine intervention to get us to see that we're supposed to be together." I drop my head, feeling my cheeks flush. "So, I guess what I'm saying is, I don't want you to be my fake boyfriend anymore. I'm not sure it was ever really fake for me anyway. I've always loved you. I think it just took removing the blinders to see it." I look up and smile softly at him.

He holds my face in his hands. "You are mine. Always have been. I've tried to tell you so many times, but it just didn't come out right. Like, remember your seventeenth birthday and I gave you that book with that note inside?" He shakes his head but smiles.

"Yeah, I love that book," I place a hand over his on my face.

"That was my immature self telling you I was in love with you. And then when I said it to your face when you thanked me for it, you replied that you loved me, too, but I don't think you understood what I was saying, and then I got too chickenshit to make it clear. Then I thought maybe it was your way of putting me in the friend zone, and rather than lose you, I accepted it. Being around you in any way was worth it." He takes my hand and kisses my palm.

"I definitely didn't realize that's what you were saying. As you know, I was pretty naive, and I had never had a boyfriend. I knew I loved you, but I don't think I realized then what it meant. Does that make sense?"

He nods. "Yeah, I mean, I think I've been in love with you for a long time before I realized what being in love meant. So, even though it hasn't been fake for me, I just want to be really fucking clear here—you are mine now. For real. No more pretending, no more hiding my feelings to keep our friendship safe. I want everyone to know you're mine, and, Noelle … I have no intention of ever letting you go."

"Well, that's good because I have no intention of letting you go either. I'm sorry it took me so long to figure it out." A few tears fall again, but it's because I'm happy this time.

"Come here." He takes hold of the back of my neck and pulls me into him. "I love you, so much that I can hardly breathe sometimes." He kisses my lips softly.

"I love you too, Casey." I kiss him this time, shifting in my seat so I can get closer to him. I wrap my arms around his neck, one hand sliding into his hair and pulling him to me. I slide my tongue into his mouth, deepening the kiss.

He breaks the kiss and slides his seat back. "I need to feel you."

He reaches for me, and I unbuckle my seat belt and climb over the console and onto his lap.

Our lips meet, but this kiss is hungry. He sucks on my tongue, and I swear I feel heat straight down to my pussy.

"Casey," I pant, intense pulses radiating throughout my body.

His erection is straining through his jeans, and as I grind down on him, the friction from the seam of mine makes me feel like I'm losing control. I don't even know that I would care if someone walked by and saw us right now.

His hands slide under my shirt, and he pulls the cups of my bra down below my breasts. When he lifts my shirt and pinches my nipples, I nearly come. He pulls back from our kiss and takes a nipple into his mouth and sucks.

"That feels so good," I say, grinding down harder on him.

He releases my nipple, but both hands cover my breasts, his thumbs rubbing my peaked nubs. "How did I get so lucky? You're perfect, Noelle. Perfect for me." He releases my breasts and runs his hand down my stomach to the button of my jeans. "Sit up a little for me."

I lift my hips as he unbuttons my jeans and pulls the zipper down. When his hand slides into my panties, I moan. "Holy shit, Casey."

"You're so wet for me, pretty girl. Let me feel you fall apart on my fingers." He pumps his index finger into me while rubbing my clit with his thumb.

"Give me your lips, Casey. I need you to kiss me." I lean down as he tilts his head up. Placing my hand on the side of his face, I slant my mouth over his, my tongue sliding over his lips, tasting him, before tangling with his.

He wraps his other arm around my waist, guiding my hips up and down on his hand. He sucks on my bottom lip, then releases it with a pop. "Are you gonna come for me like this? Or do you want my cock?"

The logistics might be challenging, but I'm up for it. "Cock. Definitely cock."

His hand slides out of my pants, and I lean my hip against the center console for balance as Casey helps me push my jeans over my hips enough so I can pull at least one leg out. Not the most comfortable position, but I can't wait. I need him now.

I reach down and unbutton his jeans, lifting my body off of him as much as I can so he can adjust his hips to slide his jeans down his legs. The head of his cock is already peeking out of his boxers. I help pull them down, and his cock springs free. I grip him in my hand, straddle him, and line his erection up with my pussy.

"Fuck," he groans. "I'll never ever tire of seeing you dripping for me." He's watching us come together as I sink down onto his cock.

For a minute, I just sit there and feel him inside me. Being with Casey like this leaves no doubt in my mind that he'll be mine forever. The way he watches me, the way he touches me … makes me feel wanted. And loved.

His hips start to thrust. "I can't hold it. I gotta move, baby."

This is the first time he's called me *baby*, and I'm a fan. Everything just feels like *more* today. Could be because of what happened at the bar with Trey, but I don't think that's the only reason. Our conversation in this car makes me feel connected to him on a whole new level.

"Casey, don't stop." I grind down, meeting his thrusts.

"You gonna come for me? Soak my cock?" His hands are on my hips, squeezing, but it feels good.

I lean down to kiss him, and it changes our position, and the friction on my clit nearly sets me off. "Fuck, Casey." I suck his tongue into my mouth as our hips roll.

He moves his mouth to my neck, kissing, sucking. "I could stay inside you, just like this, all fucking day." He nips my earlobe. "I'm not gonna last much longer. Come for me, baby."

I sit back up, feeling him deeper again. "I'm so close," I pant. "Don't come yet. Wait for me."

"Always." He reaches down between us and strokes my clit. "That's it. You're so fucking pretty. The way you take me, the way you look when you come, you look like a goddess. You look like mine."

One hand is on his chest, and the other is on the window. I feel like I'm about to lose control.

"Casey!" I drop my head back. "I'm coming! Come with me. Now!"

I look down at him, taking his face in my hands. Our eyes are locked as the first pulse of my orgasm hits.

He sucks in a breath and groans, "Fuck! I can feel you coming. Can you feel me, baby? Can you feel me claiming this pussy?" He keeps rubbing my clit as we both come.

My breaths become unsteady as a whole new level of loving this man hits me. I don't ever want there to be a time that he's not with me. I wouldn't survive it.

"Casey, I love you so much; it hurts."

"I don't want it to hurt, pretty girl. I want it to consume you, like you consume me." One of his hands slides into my hair. "You're everything to me. Always."

I bend down to kiss him as my orgasm fades. I never want to stop kissing him.

He pulls back and kisses one cheek, then the other. "I swear, I couldn't love you more. Then tomorrow comes, and I love you even more. Every day, it's like that for me. I guess that's what happens when you fall in love with your best friend."

"Casey, you're gonna make me cry." I kiss him.

"I never want to make you cry, pretty girl. It's my job to only make you smile." Both of his hands cup my face as he kisses me.

The thing with Casey is, I believe what he says because his actions match his words. I could never trust Trey because he never treated me the way Casey does. I knew what it felt like to be loved by Casey in a friendship way, but being loved like this … I never want it to end.

CHAPTER
TWENTY-FOUR

CASEY

DESPITE LOSING in the first round of the playoffs, I've never been happier. Coach commended me on stepping it up when the guys got down. Keeping your head in the game isn't easy, especially with the stakes of playing for Walker. As the season ended, Coach said my senior year looked promising and that he had big plans for me. I'm more of a lead-by-example kind of leader though, so I'm not sure what he means.

Once Noelle and I became an actual couple—officially at least since, in my head, we'd been together long before she realized it—we haven't spent a night apart. She's either at my place or I'm at hers, and somewhere along the way, "your place" and "my place" blurred into "ours."

Winter brought in a steady rhythm of classes, workouts, and stolen nights together. During the holidays, we stayed on campus, only going home for Thanksgiving and Christmas, but even then, we split our time between both families. To say her parents are ecstatic about our new relationship is an understatement.

Noelle's birthday lands just before Christmas, and I wanted

her all to myself, which is another reason we didn't rush home. Chelsea went back for the break, so we had her apartment entirely to ourselves. New Year's brought my roommates back, and we rang it in with them, champagne and all.

Meanwhile, Beck had been grinding through the winter with early mornings in the weight room, afternoons running drills, nights studying film. As the combine approached, he treated every workout like it was his ticket to the league.

I'd been training with him to keep myself in shape mostly. It was also nice to spend some time with him before he leaves once the draft is over. He'll always be a part of my life, but he's been in my life every day since he moved to Troy when we were kids. It'll be weird when he's gone. And my sister, too, since she'll go with him eventually.

After one of our workouts, we took the long way home, and we talked about what our futures would look like.

"Case, I know this isn't a surprise to you, but I'm gonna marry Charlie. I don't really care when. Fuck, I would marry her today if she let me. You know she's my endgame, and I can't live a day without her." He tapped his fingers on the steering wheel in his truck.

"Yeah, I know."

"I guess I just want to make sure we're good. You're my best friend, and I'm pretty sure you would have kicked my ass by now if you didn't want me with your sister, but I just need to know you're okay with all of it." He looked at me sincerely.

"Are you asking me for my blessing? Because I feel like that's something you need to talk to my parents about, no?" I smirked.

He nodded slowly. "I will for sure, but like I said, you're my best friend and her twin brother, man. It's important to me—and I know to her—that you're happy for us."

I put my hand on his shoulder. This wasn't the conversation I expected to have, but I'm deeply honored he thought about me. "Of course, Beck. I literally couldn't have picked a better man for my sister. I'm really happy for you both."

"Okay, cool, because I'm gonna ask her to marry me the day of the draft." His smile spread slowly.

"Naturally, because emotions won't be high enough that day." I *laughed, but reached out my hand for a handshake and pulled him in for a hug. "Congrats, brother."*

Beck isn't a spur-of-the-moment kind of guy. He'd been planning the proposal down to a T.

Spring came fast. Then Beck went to the combine, impressed every scout in the building, and kept training right up until today—draft day. We're all at his dad's house, the TV tuned to the coverage. It's strange, knowing I won't be suiting up with my best friend again. But he's not really leaving, especially since, in a few hours, he's planning to propose to my sister.

He's surprising her at the tree we used to race to at our elementary school. It has meaning to them, and I really couldn't be happier. He's like a brother to me as it is, in all the ways that count.

I'm standing in the kitchen, getting some snacks, when Noelle comes up to me and wraps her arm around my waist.

"I'm dying, Case. I wish we could be down there with them." She has a big smile on her face, and she's bouncing on her toes.

"Okay, guys, Charlie just ran out of the house! It's go time!" my dad yells from the family room.

My mom sent her home to get something she *forgot* for Beck. I don't know the details, but Beck left her a note, telling her to meet him at the tree.

I pull Noelle into me and lean down to kiss her. "You're about to see it, it sounds like. Come on."

I take her hand and follow my family and Beck's outside the house. Bo and Silas are here, too, and they follow us out.

"I can't believe they're getting engaged, bro. What's with our friends proposing on draft day?" Bo shakes his head. "I think I'll be too tied up with nerves to be thinking about anything else."

"Well, considering you don't have a girlfriend, I think you'll be fine." Silas smacks him on the chest and laughs.

"Yet. I don't have a girlfriend yet. And it's not because I can't. I just haven't found the right girl." He shoves Silas playfully.

"Yeah, yeah. So you say."

We've gotten closer to Silas this year, and he's easily become one of my best friends. He fits in well with Archie and Liam too.

They came back to Walker a few weeks ago for a visit. We hadn't seen Liam since the summer before the school year. He had transferred to Michigan in hopes of starting as their QB since Bo had taken his spot at Walker. They didn't win the championship, but they got further than we did. He declared for the draft, so we'll be watching him today too.

We all stand in the middle of the street with a view of Charlie and Beck. We're too far to hear anything, but when we see Beck get down on one knee, I hear a sniffle. Noelle is standing in front of me, my arms around her waist. I lean over to look at her. Her hands are covering her mouth, and a tear falls from her eye.

"You okay, pretty girl?" I kiss her cheek, wiping away the tear.

"I'm just so happy for them. I feel like I've had a front-row seat to their relationship, and I'm just so…happy." She hiccups the last word.

Silas looks at me, eyes wide, brows raised.

I roll my eyes and smile at him, then bend down again and kiss my girl on the top of her head. "I'm happy for them too."

"They're just, like, so in love, you know." She brings her hands to her chest.

"Baby, are you okay?" I turn her in my arms.

She can get emotional from time to time, but this seems to be making a big impact.

She nods and tilts her head to kiss me. "Yes, totally. Sorry, I'm just in my feels. I don't think I've ever seen someone get engaged before either."

My mom and dad, Beck's dad and sister all start cheering, so I look up and see Charlie jump into Beck's arms. Noelle turns and starts clapping and cheering along. I'm not gonna lie; I'm a bit more emotional than I'm letting on. There's a lot going on today. But I'm excited for my sister and my best friend. I put my fingers in my mouth and whistle.

Beck has my sister on his back as they get back to us. "All right, let's go do this thing."

He drops her, and my parents envelop her in a hug. I take Noelle's hand in mine, and we walk over to them.

While my mom sniffles and my dad tries to pretend he's not also crying, I reach my hand out to Beck and pull him in for a hug. "Congrats, man. I'm so happy for you guys."

"Thanks, brother. You're gonna be my best man, right?" So typical Beck.

Me? I breathe in deep to keep myself together. I'm not a crier, but again, this is a big day for both of our families. And this is my twin sister we're talking about. She's literally the other half of me.

"You don't have to even ask, man. You know I'll be there." I pull him in again. "Love you, buddy."

"Love you too." He laughs and smacks my back. "Come on, everyone. I need to get inside."

My sister bounces up to me, and I lift her up in my arms.

"Case! I'm getting married!" she squeals.

"I know! I'm so happy for you, Char. Love you." I squeeze her a little tighter. A bond like ours is special. "Take care of each other."

She releases me, and I let her go. "Always."

Her smile is probably the biggest I've ever seen it. She's literally glowing. Beck's hand is reaching for hers, so she takes it, but turns back to look at me.

"And I love you too, little brother." She winks at me.

Brat.

NOELLE

This is the wildest day I think I've ever had. Seeing Charlie and Beck get engaged made me feel all the things. Then the anticipation and the stress of waiting for Beck to get the call are nearly more than I can handle.

But it's all gotten me thinking about what this life will be like. Casey and I haven't really talked about what's next, but I know I'll go anywhere with him. He's staying at Walker to play one more year though, so we have some time to figure it out.

I'm sitting on Casey's lap in a chair in Beck's dad's living room, the big screen of the television practically in our faces.

"What are you thinking about?" Casey kisses my neck.

I tilt my head, touching his with mine. "Next year. What it will be like for you."

"Oh, yeah? Well, probably pretty similar to this." He laughs.

"I guess so, huh?" I smile. "Do you think about where you would like to go? I know you don't have a whole lot of control over it, but still, any thoughts?"

"Not really. I mean, it would be great to play with one of my friends, but I'll also go wherever they pay me and I can get some kind of guarantee that I'll get some playing time." He shrugs. "What about you? Do you think about where you want to be?"

"Me?" I twist in his lap and point to myself.

"Yeah. I mean, I want you to be happy wherever we go. Because make no mistake, I want you with me." He pecks my lips.

"I haven't really thought about it other than I'll go where you go. I can teach anywhere. I'll just need to get the state certifications." I lift a shoulder.

Beck's phone rings before Casey says anything else. The room quiets as Beck answers.

"Hello?" Beck smiles, which is kinda … rare. "This is he." He reaches behind himself, and Charlie grabs his hand. "Yes, sir. Looking forward to it. Thank you, Mr. Poles."

Charlie stands then, arm around Beck's waist.

Beck's dad is whispering to Charlie's dad, both excited.

"Chicago," Casey says in my ear.

I turn to look at him. "How do you know?"

"The general manager just called him." He winks at me.

As soon as Beck hangs up, his sister, Brooke, asks, "Well?"

"Beckham, we need you to sit back down or stand, whatever you want to do, but we're about to go live here." The production assistant has a clipboard in hand and points to the couch.

Charlie pulls Beck to sit next to her on the couch. His dad is on the other side of him.

"And we're live in five, four, three, two, one."

The commissioner comes on the television and introduces a veteran player from the Chicago Bears to make the announcement. Beck is the fifth pick in the first round of the draft. We all jump up and cheer. Everyone hugging and congratulating him.

The rest of the day goes by in a blur. We stay at Beck's dad's until after Liam Pitz was called. He went late in the first round to the New Orleans Saints. We saw Archie and Emma were there with him and his family. Casey, Beck, Bo, and Charlie FaceTimed with them after.

In Casey's truck, on the way back to campus that evening, I'm lost in thought, staring out the window. In just a year, everything has changed so much. And in another year, it will change again in a big way.

"You okay?" Casey reaches over and takes my hand.

I turn to face him. "I'm good. Just thinking about today."

"Yeah, it was a lot. Sometimes, I feel like we just finished middle school. And now we're making big-time decisions. Kind of wild, right?" He laughs.

"It really is. Like, things have changed so much this year. In the very best way, of course." I lean over and kiss his cheek. "And then next year, it will change again."

"You know, we've never really talked much about the future, other than us being together, but what do you want out of our life together? Do you want to have kids? When would you want to get married? Stuff like that."

"Oh, yeah, I think about it all the time now." I laugh. "I mean, that sounds kind of weird, and I have always wanted kids, but I think since we've been together, it's been on my mind more, I would say."

"Good. I think about it a lot too. Hell, I think we should just do it today." He brings my hand up to kiss it.

"Today, huh?" I smile and squeeze his hand.

He nods. "Yep," popping the *P*.

"Honestly, I would too. But I feel like we should get through next year first. Don't you?" I ask.

"I guess if we must." He sighs and rolls his eyes.

"Okay, let me ask you a question. Since you brought up babies, how many do you want?" I smile at the thought of a little Casey running around.

"However many you want to give me, pretty girl. I do hope we don't have twins, although I don't think it works like that anyway. But I can't imagine how crazy it must have been for my parents with me and Charlie. With me going pro, I wouldn't want you to have to manage that on your own with my schedule." He turns and winks at me.

"That's very thoughtful of you." I giggle. "I think twins would be fun in a way, but, yeah, a whole lot of work. Bless your mom."

"Seriously. She's a saint." He huffs.

"It would be nice to have one of each, but I'm not really

picky. Whatever life gives us, I'll just be happy because it's with you." I lean over and rest my head on his shoulder.

"I love you, Noelle James." He kisses the top of my head.

"And I love you, Casey King."

I meant what I said too. As long as I'm with him, I'll take whatever comes.

CHAPTER
TWENTY-FIVE

NOELLE

THE ELEMENTARY SCHOOL I work at is taking a field trip today to a Walker University baseball game. Am I looking forward to it? Absolutely not. What's worse is, we're scheduled to go onto the field after the game for the kids to meet the players.

Our seats are directly behind the dugout, about six rows back. The kids are so excited, and I'm trying to focus on getting them settled rather than pay attention to who is on the field. The game is supposed to start soon, and both teams are warming up right now.

Out of the corner of my eye, I see Trey warming up on the mound, but I don't think he's seen me. I really hope he hasn't. The last thing I want is for him to think I'm here for him. Because he would.

The teams are called back to their dugouts, and the announcer asks everyone to stand for the national anthem. So, I stand and instruct the kids to stand as well. When the music starts, I take a minute to look at Trey, whose back is to me. I haven't seen or heard from him since the day Casey punched him. And I don't feel any pain, seeing him, but I do feel sad that I wasted so much time with him.

Just as the song ends, I see a couple coming down the stairs to my left. I recognize them quickly as Trey's mom and dad. I met them a few times when they came to town for games, but didn't really spend much time with them. I'm not even sure they'd recognize me, honestly.

Behind them is a blonde holding a toddler. I don't recognize her, but she seems to be with his parents. They take their seats two rows back from the dugout. I look back to the field to see Trey waving to them.

The toddler is bouncing in the woman's arms, and clear as day, I hear him shout, "Dada!"

I look back at Trey, who has a genuine smile on his face when he walks to the railing. The girl leans down, and Trey reaches up to kiss the little boy, then kisses the girl.

What the actual fuck?

He says something to his parents, then looks away and makes direct eye contact. With me. The look on his face is how he should have looked when I caught him with Zoey. His eyes grow wide, and he turns around quickly.

I think I'm gonna be sick.

The girl sits next to his parents, and the toddler stands on her legs, clapping and bouncing to the music playing. He's wearing a little jersey with Trey's number on it. Then Trey's mom reaches for the boy, and when she turns him to face her, I see his face. He's an exact replica of Trey.

This cannot be happening right now. How is this even possible? That baby has to be at least a year and a half old. I'm frozen in my seat as the game starts. Thoughts run through my head, trying to piece together what I'm seeing.

We were together for nearly two years. We broke up a few times here and there, but never for any long period of time.

I can't take my eyes off the baby as I think. I want to know everything, but I also don't. Because I'm afraid of the answers if I find out.

I need to get out of here for a minute. I can feel my panic rising with every breath I take.

Leaning forward, I get the attention of my mentor. "I need to run to the restroom."

She nods.

"Oh! I have to go potty too, Miss Noelle." One of the girls in the class grabs my hand.

"Me too!" another one says.

Great. There goes getting a minute to get myself together.

"Okay, any girl who has to use the restroom, follow me." I stand and take the stairs, turning to get a head count to see who is following me. I glance to the dugout and see Trey watching me just before he looks away.

The four little girls who followed me are using the restroom, and I'm standing at the sink, looking in the mirror. I shake my head to focus since I have kids with me. God forbid one of them walks out and I don't notice. So, I splash some water on my face, then grab a paper towel to dry it.

As I'm tossing the paper into the wastebasket, the door opens. It's the blonde and the little boy. He's mumbling, and she's nodding and smiling.

"Dada, ball. Dada, ball." He claps his hands. He notices me and waves. "Hi."

I smile and wave back. "He's a cutie," I say to the girl.

"Thank you. He is cute, but he's stinky! You need a new diaper, don't you, Hank?" She kisses his cheek.

"Let me guess. Named after Hank Aaron?" I smile. That's Trey's favorite all-time player.

"Ha! How did you guess? His daddy picked it. I had very little say." She sets him on the changing table and pulls a diaper and wipes from her backpack with one hand, the other hand on Hank's belly, holding him in place.

I know I shouldn't, but I just need to know. I need to know I'm not wrong. "Is that his dad's number he's wearing?"

"Sure is! He's a pitcher for Walker." She turns to me and smiles.

The thought that this girl is talking to me right now with a smile on her face makes me feel sick. She seems so happy. So proud. There's no way she knows who I am.

"Dada, ball!" Hank babbles.

"That's right, Hank. Dada, ball." She laughs. "He's obsessed with balls. And his dada."

"That's really sweet," I whisper.

One of the little girls in my class calls to me, "We're all done, Miss Noelle."

They're all lined up by the door.

"You all washed your hands?" I didn't even notice.

"Yes, ma'am," they say together.

"You a teacher?" the blonde asks.

"Um, yes. Or, well, I will be. We're on a field trip today with the class I'm student teaching this year." I walk to the door.

"That's fun. Have a good time!" she calls out as she finishes changing Hank's diaper.

"Bye-bye!" Hank babbles.

"Thanks. You too. Bye, Hank." I wave to him. Suddenly feeling really sad for that little boy. Because none of this deception is his fault.

After the longest game in history, we make our way down to

the field for the kids to have baseballs signed, get a few pictures, and meet the players. I stand toward the back, as far away from Trey as I can possibly get.

During the game, I couldn't take my eyes off of his family. Clearly, his parents had to have known about this when they met me those few times. But who knows what he said to them about who I was? I mean, we practically lived together for two years since he stayed at my apartment all the time, but maybe he didn't talk about me. My parents certainly knew who he was.

The other thing that I stewed about was the fact that his friends had to have known. And what's worse is they all acted like they liked me. They were friendly to me while lying to my face. I feel betrayed by not just Trey, but his friends who I thought were mine too.

Some of the players, including Trey, are hugging family members and girlfriends. Trey is holding Hank in his arms, and seeing them together makes me want to cry. Trey looks happy and undoubtedly loves that little boy.

A few of the guys pass by me and nod. I can't even muster a smile in return. Liars. All of them.

The stadium operations coordinator comes over to us and directs us to an area in the outfield. As the kids follow, I stay in the back to make sure none of the kids wander off.

I feel a pull on my elbow.

"Noelle, wait." Trey is at my back, speaking close to my ear. "I just want to talk to you for a minute."

I turn to face him. "You cannot be serious."

"Yeah, I am serious. Let me explain."

His hand is still on my elbow, and I yank it away.

"No, Trey."

I turn to walk away again, but he grabs my hand this time.

"Noelle, come on."

"I met your son today, Trey. In the restroom. Hank's adorable. Really. What is he, like one and a half?" I fold my arms across my chest.

"You met him? How?" He puts his hands on his hips and leans in closer to me. It's obvious he doesn't want anyone to hear us.

"They came into the restroom when I was in there with some students. He needed a diaper change. The mom—what's her name?" I tilt my head to the side.

"Faith," he mumbles.

I can't help but laugh. "Faith?"

"Come on, Noelle. Don't make a scene." He's so close to my face that he's practically spitting in it.

"I mean, how can you not see the irony here? Does Faith believe you've been faithful to her? Does she go to school here?" I lift my hands.

"No, she was my girlfriend in high school, and she got pregnant, so she stayed home instead of coming with me to school." He huffs.

"So, what, you just saw them whenever you felt like it? How? When? We were together since our freshman year, Trey." I feel like I might cry, but I will not give him the satisfaction.

"We made it work the best we could. Why does it matter to you? I was with *you* all the time."

He reaches for me again, and I step back.

"I'm sorry. Please tell me you aren't insinuating that I'm the reason why you didn't see your baby!" I hold up my hand.

"You were so needy all the time, so, yeah, I spent more time with you. Besides, King was always sniffing around, and I wasn't about to let him take what was mine." His jaw is clenched.

"You know, Casey tried to warn me about you. After the first time he met you, he told me he didn't trust you. But I was so fucking stupid to believe every single lie that came out of your mouth. And the *I love yous*, which also came with criticism. The horrible way you manipulated, gaslighted, and made me second-guess myself all the time. You loved to tear me down and basically had me thinking I was the one doing you wrong. That I needed to be better. Do better. For you. When really, all along, you never deserved me or my time. You definitely didn't deserve my love or my body. I gave you every first I had. And you … lied the whole time. You made me the other woman." I stop, my breathing shallow. "It's taken me being loved by someone real. Someone who would never lie to me. Or hurt me to make himself feel better. To believe that I'm worth the kind of love he has to give me. I feel sick to think I gave you that power over me."

"You think he never lied to you? That's cute. Did he tell you how he felt about you? Did he ever tell you about the time he came over and threatened me?" Trey laughs.

"Whatever you're trying to do here, just stop. Everything that comes out of your mouth is a joke. And honestly, I feel sorry for Faith, but mostly, I feel sorry for your little boy. Because he's going to grow up with you as his role model. For his sake, I hope you do better." I shake my head. "Be better, Trey." I turn and walk away and back to my group.

I hear someone ask him if everything is okay, but I don't turn back to see who it is. I keep walking because I think this is it. This is the moment I puke. I've tried holding it in the entire game. But I'm not sure I can anymore. My mentor looks at me, question in her stare, but I shake my head and make my way off the field.

I barely make it to the trash can just outside the gate before I puke.

CHAPTER
TWENTY-SIX

CASEY

WHEN NOELLE TOLD me they had a field trip today to watch the baseball team play, I almost bought a ticket, just to be there for support. Not that I worry about her feelings for Trey or anything. I just know that's one of the last places she would want to spend her day.

So, I'm getting concerned that I haven't heard from her when I know the game is over. I've texted a few times with no response, which is unlike her to completely ignore me.

I'm sitting on the couch, scrolling through channels, eyeing my phone next to me. I considered going over to her place to wait for her, but she is supposed to come here when she's done.

Bo walks into the room and sits in the chair next to the couch.

"Sup, man?" He nods at me.

"Hey, what's up?" I answer dryly.

"You okay?" He leans forward and braces his elbows on his knees.

"Yeah, I'm good. I'm just waiting for Noelle to text or call, and it's just taking longer than I thought it would. I'm getting worried, is all." I look from the television to Bo.

"Is she coming over?" he asks.

"She's supposed to come over after a field trip with her class today," I explain.

"Where did they go? Maybe the bus got delayed or something." He sits back in the chair.

"They went to a Walker baseball game." I look at him pointedly.

"Oh shit." Bo puts his hands behind his head, leaning back.

"Yeah. I'm sure she's fine, but I'll feel better when I hear back."

He leans up and nods to the window. "Looks like she's pulling up now."

I jump up and leap over the couch. I'm pulling the door open and making it halfway down the walkway before she even gets out of the car. When she looks up, I can tell she's been crying. Fuck.

"Hey! I was getting worried about you." I wrap her in my arms when I reach her.

"Sorry I didn't text. I just … needed some time to think." Her arms are wrapped loosely around my waist.

I kiss the top of her head. "It's okay. What's going on?"

She laughs humorlessly. "I'm honestly not sure if you'll believe it. I think I'm still trying to wrap my head around what I saw today."

I pull back to look at her face, but I don't let go of her. "What do you mean? What did you see?"

"Let's go inside. Is anyone home?" She reaches for my hand.

"Bo is here, but Charlie is at the sorority house, and Silas is … I have no idea, honestly."

Beck has already left for Chicago, and it's been weird, not having him in the house.

"Okay, let's go into your room, and I'll tell you." She starts walking, and I follow.

When we get into the house, Bo stands from the chair. "Hey, Noelle. How's it going?"

"Hi, Bo." That's all she says.

"I'm gonna go out for a bit. Do you guys need anything?" he asks, already walking toward the door.

I shake my head. "Nah, I'm good. Thanks."

When he leaves, we walk into the kitchen, and she lets go of my hand and reaches into the fridge to grab a bottle of water.

"What's going on, pretty girl? Talk to me." I stand in front of her and cup her face. I'm trying to get her to look at me, but she won't make eye contact.

"Can I ask you something first?" She finally looks at me.

"Of course. Anything." I rub my thumbs across her cheeks.

"Did you ever go over to Trey's and threaten him?" She doesn't look mad, more like curious.

I stare at her a beat before I answer—because I want to be thoughtful with my response. "Yes, I did."

"When? Why?" She takes hold of my wrists.

I drop my head back, and her hands fall from my wrists, then I slide my hands down her arms. "Because he didn't treat you right."

"Casey, tell me what happened," she pleads.

"It was our freshman year, and it was one of the times you had broken up. When I came to see you, I overheard you telling your friends that he had been telling you to lose weight and that he didn't like your hair either." I shake my head. "You stopped talking when I came in the room, but I couldn't let it go. I could tell you were upset, but you wouldn't tell me why. But what I heard just kept playing in my head on repeat. So, later that night, after I left your dorm, Beck and I went over to his apartment. I didn't lay a hand on him, but I did tell him to leave you alone. He started spouting off about how you were his and that I was jealous. He definitely tried to provoke me into hitting him, but Beck held me back. A few days later, you were back together, so I didn't think it mattered if I told you or not."

"But why didn't you just tell me?" She tilts her head. "If that's all that happened, you could have told me that."

"Noelle, I swear that's all that happened. If he said otherwise, that's just another lie to add to the long list." I bend slightly to look in her eyes so she knows I'm being truthful.

"I believe you. And I actually remember that night I was talking to my friends about that. It was one of the first times he did that. When we got back together, he blamed me for overreacting and said my friends were trying to break us up. I thought he meant my roommates, but I guess he meant you too." She sighs. "Let's go to your room so I can tell you the rest."

As we walk down the hall, I try to put together how and why they had this conversation at the game. It makes no sense.

Noelle sits on the bed, leaning back on her hands. "I don't even know where to start."

She tells me about seeing Trey's family, and then she drops a bomb. When she starts to talk about the baby, I'm literally stunned speechless. I knew he was a son of a bitch, but this is a whole different level of scum.

When she finishes, she's not crying, but I notice her hands in her lap are shaking. I hate him for so many reasons, but I hate him the most for what he's done to her. She didn't deserve any of this. She thought she loved a man who loved her. She wanted to believe she was important to him. And all along, he had a baby with another girl. A baby he neglected by spending all his free time with Noelle.

"So, yeah, that's all of it."

I sit down next to her and wrap my arm around her shoulders. She leans into me, but she's holding back.

"I can't imagine what's going through your head, and I don't want to make assumptions. But I want you to know that you can say anything to me. Even if it's something I might not want to hear. Yes, I'm your boyfriend, but I'll always be your best friend too." I kiss her temple.

"Honestly, I can't even narrow it down to one feeling or emotion. I'm completely disgusted by his behavior for sure. I feel sad for that little boy and his mother." She shakes her head. "I'm mad at myself for being so blind. For letting him make me doubt myself, and I'm mad that I didn't see it until it was too late. I'm mad that I said and did things just to keep the peace, out of fear he would break up with me. For, quite literally, being the other woman. It's just … a lot to take in."

"Noelle, none of this is your fault. Please believe that. Trey behaved and acted selfishly, deceitfully, and I'm sure you see it by now, but he's a narcissist."

"It was so weird, seeing him with his son. The look on his face, the love that was showing, seemed real." Her hands twist in her lap.

"And I hope that's true, for his son's sake. I hope his son is the exception to the way he treats other people, but, Noelle, Trey will destroy that family in one way or another. And that is not your fault."

"I know that logically. I got to thinking though." She drops her head, closes her eyes, and takes a deep breath.

I have a feeling I'm not going to like what she's about to say. "Tell me."

When she looks up at me, tears swim in her eyes. "I think I need to go to therapy, Case. Everything with us has been so good, but I don't want it to be a Band-Aid. All of this today has made me realize just how much damage he's done to my mental health. And I feel like in order to be the best partner to you that I can be, I need to take some time to heal."

"Okay, then let's do it. We'll get you a good therapist who can work on all of this with you, and of course you have me. I'll be there to help." I take her shaking hands in mine.

"Case, I know you want to be there, but you can't always fix me or take care of the problem. I need to learn how to do it on my own. Because the fact is, I want to be able to be there for you in the same ways you're there for me. Mentally and emotionally. I want to trust myself, have confidence in myself, not because you support me, but because I believe it down to my core." The tears are streaming down her face now.

My stomach drops, and my first instinct is to say no. I want to be selfish and assure her that I won't get in the way, that I can, in fact, be there to help. But that's not what she needs right now. And as much as I don't want to admit that I can't be the one to fix her, I do think counseling would be good for her.

"For the record, this is going to kill me, but I understand, and I don't disagree." I swallow down the lump in my throat. "I think it would be good for you to have an unbiased support system. But anytime you need me, just say the word, and I'm there." It's making me sick to say this to her because every instinct is telling me to fix it.

"I know you will be. We have a lot to look forward to. I just need a little time. To be clear, this isn't a breakup. Just give me time to get moving in the right direction." She kisses my lips. "Like, you can't go dating other girls while I get my head on straight."

"Not a chance. You've always been the only girl for me." My voice is hoarse from me trying not to lose it. "We'll still talk every day, right?"

She starts to cry again and hiccups. "I honestly don't know. I worry if we do, we're going to fall into our normal pattern of you fixing it."

I feel like I'm losing my girlfriend and my best friend at the same time. Since we've been friends, from middle school on, we've talked at least once a day. There's no way I'm going to be able to handle this.

"Case, this is going to be hard for both of us, but you have to trust me. Trust us. Please be patient with me." She climbs onto my lap. "I love you more than you know."

"I love you too, pretty girl. I'm not going anywhere. I'll be here, waiting for you." I place my hand on her cheek and lean in to kiss her, then rest my forehead against hers.

We sit together for what seems like hours, her head resting on my shoulder, soaking my shirt with her tears. When she says she should go, it takes everything in me not to drop to my knees and beg her to stay, to let me be with her through this.

But I don't. I walk her to her car, give her a kiss that says everything that I can't say right now with words. Because if I do, I'll break down, which will only make things harder for both of us. Once she's buckled in, I watch her drive away, my stomach in my throat.

I walk back into the house and straight to my room, thankful that no one is home right now. I slam my bedroom door, nearly making it come off the hinges.

"FUCK!" I scream until I nearly lose my voice.

I can't sit here. I can't sit here and feel sorry for myself. I need to do something to burn off some of this anger and hurt. Because this is not about me.

So, I strip my clothes and change into gym shorts and grab my running shoes. I'm out the door within minutes, and I start running. I don't stop until I can't feel my legs anymore.

CHAPTER
TWENTY-SEVEN

NOELLE

IT'S BEEN a few weeks since I forced myself to walk away from Casey. It was literally one of the hardest things I've ever had to do. Since we've been friends, my first instinct—and I think his—was to let him fix the problem.

The first two weeks, I was seeing a therapist twice a week. Until now, it was hard to see how badly I had been treated by Trey, but once I started explaining it all to her, it was worse than I'd thought. The frequency seemed like a lot at first, but the initial sessions were more like information-dumping on my part and assessments to determine my primary challenges. My therapist prefers to call them challenges rather than issues. Each session left me completely emotionally drained. It was exhausting.

I'm down to once a week now, but I have homework on the days I don't see her. After one of my sessions, my therapist suggested I journal. So, every time I had insecure thoughts or feelings, I went in the journal and wrote until the trigger came to light. I didn't see it at first, but once I started to recognize the patterns of the triggers, it became pretty obvious.

My parents have been included in a few sessions so that they understand what I'm working on. They were so upset when they learned about some of the things that had happened with Trey. But they've been so supportive, and I feel like it's made our relationship stronger.

Then she told me to start including Casey in my journal entries. Every time I wanted to reach out to him and ask for help or tell him I needed him, I would write it out instead. This has been one of the hardest parts of this process. I miss him so much.

"Why don't you start journaling to Casey?" she says as she writes something on her notepad.

"About what?"

"Well, you can start by just explaining how you feel and even what you're working on." She lifts her hand and smiles.

"Like Dear Diary?" I ask.

"Yes, exactly. A Dear Casey, if you will."

She's suggested that I not have regular contact with him right now, but I text him little updates here and there. When he texts me back, it's so hard not to keep texting and even harder not to call. I miss his voice.

In my latest entries, I've explained what exercises I've been doing in the reprogramming process. It's not been fun, but I can slowly feel the progress.

Casey,

Today was ... not all that fun. We have been working on a lot of body image stuff, which I'm coming to realize might not have been completely triggered by Trey, but he definitely didn't help it either.

Anyway, she rolled out a sheet of paper and asked me to make an outline of how I thought I looked. It felt a little crime sceney, to be honest.

Then I had to lie down on top of the tracing, and she outlined my body.

When she asked me to stand up and look at the difference, I broke down and cried. Then she made me write inside my body outline what my favorite qualities about myself were. I'm not sure which was harder—the outline or finding qualities I actually believe to be true about myself.

It's an exercise I don't necessarily want to repeat, I gotta say. And I know it was supposed to help me, but it also made me feel ashamed of myself in a way. I think because it made me feel weak. I'm sure we'll work it out more in my next session.

Anyway, I miss you more than you can imagine.

Love always,
Noelle

We did discuss it more in detail in that session after, which led to the next exercise.

Casey,
Today made me think of you so much that it hurt. We did more body image work, and it reminded me so much of the night when you made me look in the mirror and you asked me what I saw.

Well, today, I had to take a marker and write positive words on each body part I criticized. She'd had me come in the session in my bikini, so I could stand in the mirror and look at my body fully. It almost felt like an out-of-body experience. And I'll tell you a secret ... the first few things I wrote, I stole from you. Because it's hard to see myself the way you see me. So, I guess a little "fake it till you make it" won't hurt, right?

She wants me to keep working on this, minus the markers. Every day, I need to look in the mirror and say at least one positive thing about myself and my body.

I miss you, and I love you. So very much.

Noelle

I think this will be an ongoing process for me. At least for a while.

I need to retrain my brain, my therapist says. And I want to. I want to be a healthy person. But I also want to be a good partner to Casey. I need to be able to lift him up when he needs me. He can't always be the one taking care of me.

So, for now, I'll miss him while I work on myself. I know it's hard for him, too, but in the end, it will make us stronger as a couple.

CHAPTER
TWENTY-EIGHT

CASEY

DURING OUR TIME APART, Noelle has texted me from time to time, but it's usually very simple, basic check-ins. She doesn't tell me much, and when I reply, she doesn't answer. It's been … hard.

The only thing that's making it somewhat bearable is that Chelsea texts me occasionally with updates on how Noelle is doing. I don't know if it's Noelle's idea or if Chelsea understands how hard this is on us both.

I'm in Texas this weekend with my friends for Archie and Emma's wedding. Noelle should be here with me, but the last time I texted her about it, she didn't reply. I'm just disappointed she's not here.

Trying to be happy and put on a brave face hasn't been the easiest. And it's not because I'm not happy for them—because I truly am. I just want my girl with me. I want to be celebrating friends with the woman I love next to me.

The ceremony is over, and we're all in the tent they have set up on Archie's family's ranch. It's beautiful here. Rolling hills, twinkling lights everywhere. Noelle would love it.

Couples are dancing on the dance floor, and it makes me miss her so much that it hurts. I pull out my phone and text her just that. I watch my phone, like a boy obsessed, waiting to see if she reads it. She does, but doesn't reply.

I take a long drink of my beer and set the bottle on the table.

Archie's brother Aiden walks by and slaps me on the back. "You good, King?"

"Yeah, I'm good. Just getting tired. Been a long day." I huff a laugh.

"You ain't kidding. I'm beat. It was a good day though. They're happy." He stands next to my chair and folds his arms into his chest, smiling at his brother and Emma dancing.

"That they are." I smile and nod.

"I'm gonna grab another beer. You want one?" He points to my half-empty bottle.

"I'll grab one in a few. Thanks though." I tip my chin to him.

"Okay, no problem. Get out on the dance floor when this sappy song is over. Might wake you up a bit." He laughs over his shoulder.

The song ends, and I see my sister coming toward me from the dance floor. Beck flew into Dallas from Chicago for the wedding yesterday, and he and my sister have been attached at the hip since. But she's alone now, as Beck has veered off toward the bar.

"Hey, brother. What are you doing over here, all by your-self?" She takes the seat next to me.

"Just taking a break, really. You having fun?" I look at her and offer a smile.

"I am. Nice to have Beck here. I've missed him so much. The second class is over, I'm hightailing it to Chicago. I'm not a fan of being apart." She laughs.

"I miss him, too, so I can only imagine how you feel. Well, actually, I do know; I hear your sappy conversations," I tease her.

"Shut up." She laughs. "I can't help that he's madly in love with me."

"Yeah, yeah." I nod.

"Come with me for a sec." She stands and holds her hand out to me.

I look at her outstretched hand. "I'm not dancing with you."

"I don't want to dance with you. I want you to come with me." She shakes her hand.

"Okay, I'm coming." I stand and take her hand.

We walk outside the tent, into the warm spring night.

"Isn't it so pretty here? Everything feels so big, you know? The sky feels bigger, the land endless. And the horses? Just stop it. I'm obsessed." She looks up at me and smiles.

When she looks at me like this, all excited, it reminds me of when we were kids.

I nod and smile in return. "It really is great. You gonna make Beck buy you a ranch someday?"

"I mean, you never know! I could definitely get used to this." She opens her arms wide and spins.

"So, you brought me out here to talk about the view?" I smirk.

She stops spinning and comes to stand in front of me. "No, Case. I brought you out here because I'm worried about you. My heart is literally hurting. I feel like I can feel your pain and sadness, you know. I think it's the whole twin thing." She shrugs. "Have you talked to her at all lately?"

I shake my head and look down. "No, not really. Still the same. She'll text, I'll answer, then nothing. I texted her earlier to tell her I missed her, and she read it, but didn't respond. It sucks, not having her here with me."

"Well, I will say you've done a good job of being happy for them today. I don't think Archie or Emma have noticed your moping, like I have."

"I don't mean to be like this. I really am so happy for them. And I'm happy for you that you have Beck for the weekend. I miss my best friend too, by the way. It's good seeing him." I mean it too. I miss having him around. "I sort of feel like I've lost both of my best friends. Beck gone, Noelle not talking to me. It kinda blows."

"I'm sorry, Case. I really hate this for you, and I know you'll probably be annoyed with me when I say this, but this too shall pass. It might not seem like it right now, but you will get through it. And you'll be stronger because of it. Remember what Beck and I went through last year?" She takes my hand.

"Yeah, of course."

"Well, that was probably harder for me to make him stay away than it was when we broke up in high school. The pain on his face, knowing he was right around the corner, it killed me not to go to him every night. In the end though, it was the best thing we could have done for our relationship." She tugs at my hand, trying to get me to look at her. "Case, it will be okay. She'll come back to you."

I take a deep breath in. "I hope so. I mean, I can't imagine an alternative. The thing that pisses me off about the whole thing—and I'm not mad at her or upset with her. I'm mad that Trey did this to her. I'm mad that he messed her up. And I couldn't stop it. I couldn't protect her from it."

"Yeah, but, Casey, Trey will get what's coming to him. I hate to say that, but you know it's true. I hope it's not at the expense of that little boy of his though."

"I still can't believe he has a kid. Blows my fucking mind. How do you do that to a kid? To the mother of your child?" I shake my head. The whole thought of it makes me sick.

"It's absolutely awful. But, Case, he has to look at himself in the mirror every day, knowing he did that. And I'm sure he justifies it in his mind because he's a selfish prick. That boy though will figure out what kind of man his father is. And as sad as it is to say, Noelle will be one of many he does this to. Because it's not really about wanting her. It's about control and really ... his own low self-esteem. People who put others down, treat people the way he treated Noelle, are struggling with their own issues. I'm not making excuses for him. I'm just saying, the boy has issues."

"Yeah, I know all of that. I just hate that my girl is collateral damage from it. I need her to be okay, Char. It's killing me." I drop her hand and cover my eyes with my palms.

"Urgh, Case." She takes hold of my wrists. "I hate this. It hurts me to see you like this. You know she loves you though. She really does. And you have to remember that she's doing this for herself—to heal, to purge all the messages he put into her head. She's doing it for you too. You are her future, and she wants to be the best version of herself."

"I hope so. I just can't imagine any kind of life without her. She's everything to me." I drop my hands and tilt my head back, seeing a million stars in the sky.

"Casey, she'll come back to you. Be patient with her a little longer, okay?" She wraps her arms around my waist.

I hug her back, feeling the first bit of comfort since Noelle left my house that day. "I'm trying to be."

"You got this, little brother. I love you to death, and I want you to be as happy as I am. And I really believe you will get everything you want. She'll be back." She pulls away just enough to see my face. "Now let's go do some shots with our friends."

I chuckle and roll my eyes. "I don't know about shots. Give me a second, and I'll be in."

She nods and squeezes my arm as she goes back into the tent.

I stand there for a minute, looking back up at the sky. A star shoots across the sky, and I'm gonna take that as my sign that everything is going to be okay.

Pulling out my phone, I step away from the tent and turn my camera to get as much as I can in. The hills, the glow from the lights of the party, and the big sky fill the frame. I snap it and text it to Noelle. I don't text anything other than the photo. Not expecting a reply, I pocket my phone again.

"Let's go, Case. Get in here." Beck pops his head out of the tent opening. "We're doing one more round before they take off."

"I'm coming."

A spin on my heel, I walk back into the tent, but before I go in, I feel my phone buzz. When I pull it out, there's no message, but she did heart my photo. That little thing just gave me hope that we're almost there. One step closer to getting my girl back.

TWENTY-NINE

NOELLE

BEST FRIEND. It's a term we use loosely in our day-to-day lives. It's the person you hang out with the most. The one who is in close proximity. A classmate, a coworker, a family member. I know girls who have ten best friends. Guys who claim everyone on their team is their best friend. For me, I've always had a lot of friends, but only one has ever been like Casey King.

From the day I met him, Casey and I just clicked. Our jokes in sync, our interests appealing to the other, and we always had fun. When the heavy started to take hold years later—family fights, our first breakups (mine to Cade in eighth grade, his to Kayla our freshman year of high school), basic teenage angst and drama—we always ran to each other. That person you can count on, no matter what. Who can be honest when you want a lie, but deserve the truth. Who will cancel his plans on a Friday night to stay in with you because you had a fight with your boyfriend. The girl who changed her plans to watch all your football games whether she was in the stands or not.

The last few months apart from Casey have been harder than I thought they'd be. Pulling away was an impulse reaction to what had happened with Trey at the baseball park, but a strong one. It was something I knew I had to do. Not only for myself, but in order to have a healthy relationship with Casey.

I've always loved Casey. Deep down in my bones, I *love* him. Despite that internal voice knowing he was the perfect choice for me, I never felt that it was worth risking our friendship over.

While this time apart has been tragically difficult, at the same time, I feel like I'm making really good progress. So good that my therapist thinks that it would be beneficial for me to spend time with Casey.

Thank God.

I want to do this the right way. I want him to understand what I've been working on, and I also want him to know how much it means to me that he's been so patient.

After classes ended, I stayed in my apartment to finish some of the intensive therapy sessions, but now I'm down to once a week, and I drive from my parents' house back to Walker for those appointments. The boating season is upon us, and my family needs my help at the marina. They've also been support-ive, so I feel like I really need to be there for them too. Besides, I love being at the lake.

So, with Charlie and Beck's help, I'm surprising Casey. It's been so hard not to call him once my therapist made the sugges-tion to spend time with him again and even harder not driving over there and jumping his bones. I've missed him in more ways than I can count.

I'm not really sure what they've told him or how they got him here, but they're on their way. I'm waiting for him on our little patch of island we claimed years ago. It feels like the perfect place for us to come back together.

My patience is running out though, so I'm hoping they show up soon. Every boat that passes makes me jump. And I can't see the dock from here, so I have no idea when they'll get here.

I don't know many men who would put up with their girlfriend ghosting them the way I did. Part of me wonders if he changed his mind in our time apart.

Not able to sit still, I walk over to the blanket I laid out on a small patch of sand tucked into the trees. I check the basket of food for probably the thousandth time. The sun will be setting soon, too, so I make sure the little LED candles I brought with me are flickering.

Yes, I'm trying to give him the same kind of treatment he's given to me. It's about time I showed him how special he is.

After a few minutes, which really feels like an hour, I hear a boat getting closer to the shoreline. I can hear Charlie's voice over the hum of the motor.

"Stop trying to guess, Case. You're gonna ruin it. Jesus."

I can't help but let out a laugh. I've missed all of them, and I'm really sad I missed Archie and Emma's wedding. I can't wait to see all the pictures.

When I hear the boat hit sand, I walk out and to the shoreline. Beck is driving, and Charlie is standing behind Casey, who is standing at the bow, ready to jump off. He looks so good that it hurts—that beautiful, dark hair and soulful eyes. He's clad in a white T-shirt that shows off his body, which I've become all too familiar with.

He lands in the water with a splash and comes toward me. I hear Charlie speak, but I can't make out what she's saying because all I can see is him. I can tell he's holding himself back, and I hate that.

That trepidation in my belly, the one from my wondering if maybe his feelings changed on me, creeps up.

I lift my hand and smile. "Hello, Casey King."

He comes to stand directly in front of me. I want him to reach out to me, but I think he's letting me set the pace.

"Hello, Noelle James." A smile breaks out across his face. A smile that can make a girl drop her panties and her heart flutter.

"I sure have missed you." I reach for his hands.

"Not nearly as much as I've missed you, pretty girl."

He pulls me into him slowly, and just like that, the tension in my shoulders falls, and I smile so big that I'm laughing.

Seeing him, touching him—it makes me so happy. I can't help the tears that drop. I wrap my arms around his neck and lift up on my toes. Ever so softly, I kiss him. I kiss him softly, wanting to feel every minute of this kiss. It's been too long, and I want to savor it.

His hands cup my face, and he tilts his head to deepen the kiss. The pace is still slow, but more intense. When he pulls back, he kisses my cheeks, wiping my tears away with his lips.

"Thank you for coming. I wanted to call you, but I felt like I needed to show you how much you mean to me and how much it's meant to me that you gave me this time to work on myself. I know it wasn't easy for either of us."

"I will always come for you. Anytime, anywhere." He brushes his thumbs across my cheeks. "When Charlie and Beck started acting squirrelly about coming to the lake, I suspected something might be happening, but I wasn't sure what. And honestly, it didn't matter because I thought I might get to see you."

I drop my hands from his neck and take his hands in mine, leading him to the blanket. "Well, I wanted to have dinner together in our spot."

He whistles when he sees the candles lining the short path to the blanket. "This is fancy. I'm not sure it's ever looked so nice back here." He pulls me into him before we reach the blanket. "Let me just hold you for a minute. I need to breathe you in. Make sure this is real."

"It's real. I'm here with you." I wrap my arms around his waist and hold onto him like I never want to let go. Because I don't. And I won't.

Are we being a touch dramatic? Maybe. But that's what happens when you don't see your best friend—your boyfriend—for months. You hold each other. Breathe each other in.

After several minutes of holding me, he pulls back and kisses my forehead. "Did you bring food?"

I can't help but laugh. "Yes, I brought food. This is a date after all."

"A date? All right then, show me whatcha got."

He takes my hand, and we step onto the blanket. I don't even care that we're getting sand all over it.

I let go of his hand and kneel on the blanket. Inside the small cooler, I have some sandwiches, cheese and crackers, some fruit, and a few bottles of water for him and some Dr. Pepper for me.

Once I set everything out, I look up to see him watching me. I can't read the expression on his face, which is a first. "What's wrong?"

"Nothing. I just want to look at you. And I want to make sure you're okay. Are you okay?" He takes my hand.

I scoot closer to him on the blanket, and he pulls me into his lap.

I wrap my arm around him and cup his face in my hand. "I'm okay. I'm better than okay because I'm here with you."

"But can you tell me, why now? Is this just for a night?" He's searching my face, trying to read me.

I nod. "Well, now, because I've been making really good progress, and my therapist thinks, at this point in my recovery process, you'll be a positive influence. We just need to make sure I don't fall into old habits, calling you to fix everything for me." I search his eyes to make sure he's understanding me. "And, no, this isn't for a night. It's for forever."

"I want to be there for you though. So, how do we find a balance between you accepting my help because I love you and you asking for help because you want me to fix whatever it is you're feeling?"

"Have you been doing some therapy of your own?" I pull back a little to see his face.

"Not really, but I have been doing some reading on codependency. I want to make sure I can give you what you need, but also understand when I can't fix it."

I'm a little stunned. Although I don't know why. This is who he is. He cares deeply for people.

"That means a lot to me that you would do that. My therapist has also suggested that we have a few sessions together. If you're open to it."

"One hundred percent open to it. I'll do anything for you."

I turn in his arms so I'm straddling him. "Anything?"

He smirks. "Anything." His hands drift up the back of my shirt. "Is this okay?"

"Oh, yeah, more than okay. I need to feel your hands on me. It's been too long." I reach down and take the hem of his shirt in my hands and pull it up and over his head.

He pulls my shirt off and unclasps and removes my bra. His fingers trail over my chest reverently. "You're so beautiful. Inside and out." He drops his head and takes one of my nipples into his mouth.

"Ahhh," I gasp.

He moves to the other nipple, and I hold his head as he nips and sucks. Then I begin to roll my hips, feeling his erection through his shorts. His mouth parts from my nipple with a pop.

"Jesus fuck, I've missed you." His hands take hold of my hips, and he guides me back and forth over his cock. "We don't have to do anything you aren't ready for."

It's sweet, but no. I need him like I've never needed him before.

"Oh, I'm ready. For all the things. Reconnecting with you emotionally and physically. You know, I don't think you realize how much you helped me feel confident about my body in the sense of what felt good, how to feel good and not be embarrassed by it. You were so patient with me, and you knew exactly what to do and say."

"It's easy when you worship someone the way I worship you. You are everything to me. Every. Thing. I want you to see what I see, love what I love. Because it's pretty fucking incredible." He kisses me, tongue thrusting into my mouth, devouring me.

I break the kiss long enough for us to remove our clothes, so when I straddle him again, we're both naked. But I'm not in a hurry. I want to feel all of him tonight.

My tongue slides along his sensually. Our hands roam over each other's bodies, remembering every plane and curve. Hips rocking.

I'm so wet and turned on at this point that I could probably come from just the slide of his cock hitting my clit.

Sliding my hips forward, I move up his length so the crown reaches my opening. I pull back from our kiss and look him in the eye while I sit down on his cock. We both groan as we join.

"Casey, holy shit, you feel good." I breathe.

"I know, baby. You feel like heaven." His hands are guiding my hips up and down.

"I want this feeling to last forever, but I don't think I'll make it too long." I lean in to kiss him again.

He takes my bottom lip between his teeth and sucks it into his mouth.

We both begin to move faster, getting closer to reaching our orgasms. Our kiss breaks, and we're both panting, moaning against each other's mouths.

"That's it, ride me. I need to feel you come. It's been too long. Come, baby."

Just as his finger and thumb pinch my nipple, heat rips through my body—from my chest to my core. "Casey ... oh ... yes. Don't stop."

"Fuck. Fuck."

He thrusts up into me hard, then stops when he's deep inside me. My orgasm hasn't slowed, and I can feel every pulse and twitch of our bodies joined together.

After we catch our breath, I roll off of him, but I snuggle into him and rest my head on his arm, and we both look up at the sky. He's slowly running his fingers up and down my arm, and I suddenly feel like I'm going to cry, but in a good way.

I sit up and look down at his gorgeous face, illuminated by the candles and the stars in the sky. "Casey ..." I start to tear up. "I love you so much. Thank you for letting me have the time I needed, but really, thank you for loving me, flaws, insecurities, and all."

He cups my cheek and looks me in the eye. "It's my honor and privilege to love you and be loved by you. Never ever question that. You are mine, and I am yours. Always."

EPILOGUE

CASEY

FOR NOELLE'S birthday this year, I decided to combine her party with my sister's Christmas PJ party. Charlie loves to celebrate the holidays and usually plans it out for all of us. She sets up the gift exchange and everything.

This year is no different. She's specifically told everyone they have to wear funny Christmas PJs, or they can't come in the house. She takes this very seriously. But she's also helped me plan something else.

I'm going to propose to Noelle tonight. And I want everything to be perfect. I even wrote it out in my playbook, on its very own page.

Charlie usually goes to Chicago on the weekends to see Beck, but because this is such a big moment for me, she really wanted to be here. It sucks Beck can't be here, but he plays tomorrow afternoon and wouldn't have the time to come down and get back in time.

My sister, Bo, Silas, and I are in the kitchen, finishing the meal prep. Bo and Silas have come a long way with their cooking skills, and Charlie says they've become quite the sous chefs.

I'm in charge of getting the appetizers ready and set out on platters around the island in the kitchen. Every time I hear a car door outside, I look toward the front door. I'm so distracted that I almost drop one of the platters, but … wide receiver here.

"Casey, I literally can't with you right now. You're making me anxious because you're anxious. I'm feeding off your energy, and I feel like that's an unfair twin thing. Go do something while you wait for her to get here. Like go make sure none of the light bulbs on the tree have burned out." Charlie pushes me toward the family room, but I don't budge, and I lean against the island. "Bo, you finish getting the appetizers out."

"They're LED lights, Char." I huff.

"Dude, why are you so anxious anyway? Didn't she just leave a few hours ago?" Silas asks me.

They don't know what I plan to do today.

"I just can't wait for you all to see our PJs. We're totally gonna win the PJ competition."

"Hold up. There's a competition?" Silas holds up his hands. "No one told me this."

"No, Silas. I told you to be creative with your choice. And this is what you went with." She motions up and down, spoon in her hand.

"First of all, my pajamaralls are tough. Look at the detail. The caribous are banging. Literally. That shit's funny." He smirks.

"I'll give you that, but are you not going to wear a shirt under it?" My sister laughs.

He looks at her incredulously. "Why would I? This meat is prime, baby." He flexes his biceps and cracks up, which makes us all start laughing.

"Bo, I didn't see yours. What does your shirt say?" Charlie looks over her shoulder at him.

He's wearing black-and-red plaid pajama pants and a black shirt. "Uh … it says *I Have Everything I Need.*"

"Okay, cute, but also I don't get it." Charlie shrugs.

Charlie is wearing pink Christmas pajamas with Beck's face all over them. He's not even smiling in the picture, which makes it even funnier.

"Knock, knock!"

"We're in here, Brooke!" Charlie yells.

"Hey, everyone! Merry Christmas!" Brooke, Beck's sister, bounces into the room, wearing pajamaralls too. Hers have Christmas trees in a pattern on them though with a crop top underneath. Brooke is in her first year at Walker, and she spends a lot of time here at the house with us. She's like our little sister too.

"Oh. My. God. Did you two plan this?" Charlie looks between Silas and Brooke.

"What?! No!" She sets a wrapped box on the island.

"Aww, come on, Brookie. Let's tell them." Silas walks over to her and wraps an arm around her shoulders.

"As if, Silas!" Brooke pushes his arm off, but laughs.

A few minutes later, Arbor and Lily come in. Lily's boyfriend was supposed to come tonight for us to finally meet him, but it looks like he bailed on her again. They're in matching pajamas with Arbor's saying *Nice* and Lily's saying *Naughty*.

"Charlie, where do you want us to put the gifts for the exchange?" Arbor asks.

"You can go ahead and put them under the tree," she tells her.

"I brought some candy canes. Can I put those on the tree, or will that mess up your aesthetic?" Arbor asks her seriously.

"What color are they?" Charlie asks, also seriously.

"Pink, of course." Arbor puts a hand on her hip.

Charlie nods once. "Then, yes, you may proceed." Then she laughs.

"I love a pink candy cane. I'll go help," Brooke says. She picks up her gift box and follows them over to the tree.

"What up, bitches?!" A deep voice with a Texas twang rings out.

The front door slams open, hitting the wall behind it.

"You almost put a hole in the wall!" another voice whispers.

"I heard that!" my sister yells. "Which one of you did it?"

Ace and Aston Griffith, two of Archie's younger brothers, stroll into the kitchen.

"Nothing to see here." Aston snickers.

"What's up, Chuck? Smells awesome in here," Ace says as he looks over my sister's shoulder.

"Your brother is the only one who is allowed to call me Chuck." She nudges him back with her shoulder. "And both of you, go wash your hands. They're probably filthy."

They look at each other, both holding in a laugh. They have matching pants in green and red, but their shirts are different. Ace's red shirt says *Hung* with only a stocking on it. Aston's green shirt says *Come sit on my lap* with a picture of a Santa hat above it.

"Okay, Charlie, the appetizers are ready. Do you need help with anything else?" Bo turns and asks her.

"Nope, we're good. The ham is in the oven, along with the potatoes, mac 'n' cheese, and green beans and carrots." She opens the oven door, peeking inside. "We can eat as soon as Noelle and Chelsea get here."

"Am I done too then?" Silas asks.

"Yep, we're all set." Charlie wipes her hands on a towel.

"Let's go pick out a Christmas movie." Bo tilts his head to Silas toward the family room.

"Don't put on *Christmas Vacation* though. We have to watch that later when I call Beck," Charlie calls after them.

"You're gonna FaceTime him to watch the movie, aren't you?" I ask her, walking over to her and putting my arm around her.

"Uh, yeah. It's tradition to watch it together." She looks up at me and smiles. "Are you okay? You know she'll say yes, right?"

I swallow. "I mean, I think she will. We've talked about it enough that I would be destroyed if she said no." I huff a laugh.

"Case, she is crazy about you. I can't believe we're both getting married!" she squeals and wraps her arm around my waist. "We're growing up so fast." There's a huge smile on her face.

"That we are." I laugh with her and pull her into a hug. "Thanks for helping me with this."

"Always." She pushes me away. "Okay, don't make me cry."

The front door opens, and finally, my girl is here.

NOELLE

"Hey, y'all!" I yell.

Chelsea and I walk into the house, and I have a few packages in my hands.

"Happy birthday, Noelle!" everyone shouts, making me laugh.

"Aww, thanks!"

I toe off my shoes, and Casey comes over to me and takes the packages from my hands.

"Hi." I tilt my head up for a kiss.

"Hi, pretty girl." He kisses my nose, then my lips.

"Charlie, it smells so good in here," Chelsea says, walking toward the kitchen.

"Hey, girl. Thank you so much, and I agree! The food will be ready in just a few minutes." Charlie walks back over to the oven. "We have snacks and apps if you want to eat something before dinner." She stands back up and looks at Chelsea. "Love your PJs, Chels. Looks like you have a match in the house, huh?" She winks at her.

The guys are all talking about football, but I notice Bo looking into the kitchen at Chelsea.

Archie's twin brothers came to Walker this year and are on the team. Arbor, Lily, and Brooke are talking about something on Lily's phone. And *Elf* is playing on the television, even though no one is watching it.

The tree is twinkling, and lights shine all around the house. The food smells amazing. And it's loud in here with everyone talking, but the noise is comforting. I absolutely love being part of this group.

Casey sets the packages under the tree. When he walks back over to me, I can't help but giggle at our matching PJs. Our pants are black-and-white checkered, and our shirts are black with a Little Debbie Christmas Cake on the front with the words *Out here wanting to eat a snack* on his and *Out here lookin' like a snack* on mine. We're so cute. But then I notice he looks a little … nervous or something.

"What's wrong?" I ask him.

"Nothing's wrong. Why? Do I look like something is wrong?" He takes my hands in his and pulls me into his chest.

I can't help but laugh. "Case, honestly, what's your deal?"

"You know what? I can't wait." He stalks over to the tree and grabs a box from underneath.

"Casey King! Don't you dare. You'll ruin the plan," his sister yells.

I look back and forth between them.

"What's going on?" I laugh nervously.

Once he's in front of me, he takes one of my hands in his. I look around the room because I have no idea what's happening, but by the look on everyone's faces, they don't know either. But they're all watching intently now. When I meet his gaze, his look has changed into something softer, maybe even a little … shy?

"Noelle, I really want you to open your present now, if that's okay."

He holds out the box to me. I release his hand and take it in both of mine.

"Okay … now?" I raise my brows.

"Yes, please." He smirks.

I start to pull the Christmas wrapping paper from the box, and once it's unwrapped, I open the lid just as I see Casey drop to one knee.

I gasp before I even look inside the box. "Casey!"

"Look inside, pretty girl." His hands are propped on his bent knee, and he nods toward the box.

I pull the tissue paper out of the box, revealing a red ornament with the words *Will you* on the front. I can feel tears pooling in my eyes.

"Turn it around." His voice is hoarse.

I lift it by the string and turn it around to see *Marry me?*

"Casey, oh my God!" My hands are shaking, and the tears are running down my face now.

"There's one more thing in that box." He tips his head toward the box, his voice a little scratchy.

I see the ring in the box and pull it out. "Casey, it's beautiful!" I drop to my knees so we are eye to eye. Keeping the ring between my fingers, I set the box on the ground next to me.

"I'm supposed to be on my knees for you, pretty girl." He laughs.

I shake my head. "I want to look you in the eye for this." My smile is watery.

"Okay then. Let's do this." He takes my hand holding the ring and takes it from my fingers. "From middle school on, you've been my best friend. Then that friendship turned into love so deep that I can't figure out how I got so lucky to call you mine. When I think about my future, it's you standing with me. I want to keep writing this story with you. Always. Noelle James,

I love you more than words could ever say. Will you do me the greatest honor of my life and become my wife?"

"Our story is my favorite, and I want to live in it forever." I'm full-on crying, but also laughing—so many feels at once. "Yes! A million yeses! I love you so much!"

He slides the ring on my finger, and then I take his face in my hands and kiss him like there's no one else in the room.

Everyone starts to clap, and someone whistles.

When we stand, Charlie is the first to hug us. Her phone is in her hand, and Beck is on FaceTime.

"Congratulations, you guys!" Charlie says with tears.

"Baby, I can't see anything but Casey's shirt," we hear Beck say.

"Oh, sorry!" She pulls away and turns her camera toward us.

"Congrats, brother. Happy for you both." Beck smiles and gives a nod.

"Thank you," we both say.

Everyone else gathers around to congratulate us, and the girls want to see my ring. After everyone settles back into what they were doing before the proposal, I wrap my arms around Casey's neck.

"This is literally the best birthday I've ever had. Thank you for being so amazing."

"Happy birthday, pretty girl. I love you." He kisses me softly.

"I love you, Casey King." I kiss him again.

Charlie steps back into the room, hands on her hips. "Okay, so, as happy as I am for you guys, you totally ruined my time-line, Casey. I had a plan. We"—she motions between herself and Casey with her fingers—"had a plan."

"Sorry, Char. I just couldn't sit through a whole dinner, holding that in." He wraps his arm around my waist.

"Fine, whatever." She pouts, even though she's smiling. "Since we're changing things up, why don't we just have dessert before dinner and the gift exchange and sing 'Happy Birthday' to Noelle now?" She shrugs.

"I mean … I'm good with that," I say, smiling.

"Okay then. Everyone, get in here. We're singing 'Happy Birthday' first!" She spins and waves a hand over her shoulder. "Let's have some cake!"

Want to see what Casey and Noelle are up to now? Read their bonus chapter here.

Bo's story is up next. Read the first chapter from *Silent Count*.

SILENT COUNT SNEAK PEEK

Bo

Sitting in the coach's office feels like waiting for the school principal to come in and issue detention. My hands are a little sweaty, my knee is bouncing, and I keep checking the time on my watch. I think I know why I'm here, but every possible scenario runs through my mind.

Now, I'm a confident guy. I'm a leader on the field, and I like to think that carries into my personal life, as well. Things like school, sports, and friendships have always come easily to me. Don't get me wrong, I work hard, and I stay focused. I'm a doer, not a sayer.

There's just one thing that I can't quite get my head around this semester. Psychology 101. I still don't understand how my advisor missed this, but here we are. I'm in my third year, taking a first-year class.

I hear Coach talking in the hall, and then the door opens, and he shuts it behind him. *Shit.*

"Callaway." He nods, then takes a seat at his desk. "I'll get right to it, because my wife is expecting me home for dinner tonight, since I haven't been home all week to eat with her and my kids."

There's a folder sitting on the top of a stack of papers, and he takes it and sets it in front of him, then puts on his glasses. "You know why you're here?"

"I have a guess, sir." I fold my hands together, elbows on my knees. "My psychology class?"

He nods. "Son, how did you get a D on your first paper in an introductory class? You're one of the smartest kids I know. This doesn't track."

I swallow a lump in my throat before I answer. "Well, sir. I'm not exactly sure why. Honestly, I'm still shocked my advisor missed it in my freshman year. And I'm also confused about why I need it for my political science degree."

"It doesn't matter why, what matters is that it's required and you have a D right now, which is a big problem for me, son. I need you on that field for every game this season. I want that trophy again this year. And I know you want to go out strong for the draft, am I right?" He tilts his head down and looks at me over his glasses.

"Yes, sir." I nod.

"Good. So here's what we're gonna do. You'll be assigned to a tutor, and you'll establish a schedule with her around your practices and classes, while also being mindful of her availability. Am I clear?" He opens the folder and starts scanning the paperwork.

"Yes, sir, absolutely respectful of her time." I sit back and grip the arms of the chair. "Is she a TA or something?"

He shakes his head. "I believe this is a paid job for her, so really, whether you show up or not, she'll get paid, but Bo, you better be there for every single second. If that grade isn't moved up to at least a B on your next paper, I'll have to pull you, and I really can't afford to do that. Understand?" He doesn't look at me, but he takes a sticky note off a pad and starts writing.

"I understand." I scoot forward in my seat to see what he's writing.

"I'd also gather that your father monitors your grades?" He picks up the note, folds it, and hands it to me.

"That he does, sir. I'll have to let him know about this and my tutoring. It's always better if he hears things from me first." I chuckle uncomfortably and take the sticky note from him and put it in my pocket. My dad is the Chief Justice of the Supreme Court in California, and he keeps tabs on me pretty closely for multiple reasons.

"I can imagine so." He lightly smacks his hand on the table, signaling the end of our conversation. "Call this girl as soon as possible and get your time coordinated. I want an update by Friday on when your first meeting is." He stands and walks around his desk.

I take that as my cue to also stand. "Yes, sir. I'll take care of it right away."

He opens the door and stands beside it, waiting for me to leave. "See you at practice tomorrow, Bo." He holds his hand out for me to shake.

"See you tomorrow, Coach." I shake his hand and release it, then walk out the door.

I can hear one of my roommates still hanging around in the locker room, so I head in the direction of his loud voice.

"Sup, Callaway. I didn't realize you were still here. I thought you left at the same time as King." Silas finishes packing up his bag, zips it, and heads in my direction.

"Nah, I had a meeting with Coach real quick. You riding with me?" I don't really want to tell him I need tutoring right now, especially not in front of my other teammates.

"Yep, let's roll. Glad I don't have to walk home." He chuckles. "I'm hungry and I always love it when it's Charlie's night to cook." He laughs and rubs his stomach.

I hold out my fist for him to bump. "No doubt it'll be good. Her nights are by far my favorite." We live in the same house with one of our other teammates, Casey King, and his twin sister, Charlie. We all take turns making dinner one night each week and eat together. It's a nice tradition they started a few years ago when Charlie moved in.

Silas and I make the walk to my SUV, chatting about practice and some of the new plays we'll be running this season. We've been practicing for a month now, but the season is just getting started, so new plays and adjustments are usually made once the coaches see how we work together as a team.

When I get to my car, I put my gear in the backseat, then get into the driver's seat. I pull out the note from my pocket so I don't forget about it and accidentally wash it. That would be bad. I open it to stick onto my phone and see the name written on it. She just so happens to be the girl I can't stop thinking about since I met her. But she doesn't know it, because I've never made a move. She kinda intimidates me, to be honest.

Silas hops in the front passenger seat after tossing his bag in the backseat. "What's that? You get a girl's number?" He smirks.

"Uh, yeah, something like that." I quickly put the note on my phone and set it in a small compartment on the left of the wheel, out of view from Silas.

Our ride home takes minutes, and I pull up behind Casey's girlfriend, Noelle's car, on the street in front of the house. I pocket my phone, then we both grab our bags from the backseat and make our way to the door, still talking about football.

Silas walks into the house first and announces our arrival. "Daddy's home!" He drops his bag by the door, right in my path.

A round of laughter rings out. "Ew, Silas. Don't ever say that again!" Noelle calls out.

I move Silas's bag out of my way with my foot, then set my bag down next to his. When I walk around the corner into the kitchen, I stop in my tracks.

Am I dreaming? She's here. The girl I can't stop thinking about. Chelsea Sullivan. My new tutor.

WALKER UNIVERSITY STALLIONS
Counter Play
Zone Protection
Strong Side
Silent Count

ACKNOWLEDGMENTS

To my family, this one wasn't easy for me, but every time I looked at your faces, I remembered why I was doing it and pushed on. You're my reason for everything. I love you all, eternally.

Compass Press, thank you for walking me through the author journey. I promise Bo's book will come much quicker!

Jovanna Shirley, once again, thank you for your patience and expertise. I can't wait to work with you on Bo's book! And I promise I will be on time with it.

Jeannine Colette, you are amazing and bring beauty to everything you touch. Thank you endlessly for working with me on this book. And thank you for giving me the motivation to keep going and get it done!

Sarah Sentz, I'm forever grateful to you. You make my life and Autumn's so much easier. But your feedback and love for these characters go beyond what is expected or asked. Thank you for loving Casey. Your enthusiasm for him definitely kept me motivated.

Tina Otero, thank you so much for working with us to polish and shine this book baby. But mostly...thank you for your patience.

Sam R, I live for your updates when you're reading. Every tag, story, or text that is shared with me, makes my entire day. Thank you for loving this book and your incredible feedback! I can't wait to send you Bo!

To all the readers, thank you for giving me a chance and reading more of my words! Your reviews, edits, and just knowing you're reading, still blows my mind. Thank you, thank you!

Wordsmith Publicity, Autumn and Roxie, thank you for helping me reach readers and your guidance and support!

ABOUT THE AUTHOR

Ava Sutton is a sports enthusiast and author of spicy college and professional sports romance.

When she's not writing, you can find her nose in a book, scrolling social media or planning dream vacations she someday hopes to take. She lives in Dallas, Texas with her two dogs. Connect with her on Facebook, Instagram, and TikTok. @avasuttonbooks

www.avasuttonbooks.com

www.ingramcontent.com/pod-product-compliance
Lightning Source LLC
Chambersburg PA
CBHW030758200726

PP18592100001B/5